Heaven Inc.
a:1, b:1, c:1...z:1
World of Administration

Tammuz 20, 5764

Rabbi Tzvi Freeman
x: 1875.99830 y: 354.09203 z: 925.3847103
Ground Floor
World of Assiya

Dear Rabbi Freeman,

Due to the urgency of the situation, I am taking these moments from my hectic schedule to write to you personally. It is certainly understood that the contents of this letter are written in strict confidence and are not to be shared with anybody.

We at Heaven Inc. have worked since Genesis 1.1 to provide a sheltered, user-friendly environment in which earthly beings may play. We have taken great pains to be as consistent as possible with the Laws of Nature (as they are called), suspending them only when absolutely required by The Boss, blessed be He, for specified exceptional and spectacular events—for otherwise, there would be no room for human rationalism. Our employees work hard to ensure that a steady flow of both vivifying and isifying energy reach your realm on a daily basis. As you are well aware, it has been demonstrably proven that major and minor crashes, freezes and glitches originate solely through careless and often device-abusive actions of the end-users, i.e., your fellow corporeal beings.

It perturbs us, therefore, that you persist in your efforts to undermine the most critical aspect of our management scheme, namely, information protocol.

It is well known that a healthy environment can only be attained when the end-user is protected from the complexities that generate this environment. If every gamer could see the code behind each artifact of every game, the gaming industry would be pretty much down the drain.

Rabbi Freeman, certainly you would not intentionally sabotage our vital services in the same way. Yet your conduct in digging up classified documents such as were purposely and with good intent removed from public purview, and publicizing them online at Chabad.org has already caused serious damage to our protocol. Recently, information has reached us of your plans to publish these materials for distribution in the mainstream market. This is cause for even more alarm.

Surely you realize the almost certain consequences of these actions. Consider, for one moment, the devastating impact this disclosure will have upon the self-confidence of the corporeal beings. How will they continue to take pride in their puerile pastime of accumulating earthly junk if you succeed in exposing the underlying synchronicity provided by Heaven Inc.? Humankind will awaken to discover that over ninety percent of its members have been playing the game in a near passive, demo-mode, with all input generated almost exclusively from Above.

Furthermore, as you yourself have noted, a key challenge-factor of reality (as it is currently played in your realm) is the "struggle-in-the-dark" element. True, this modality has caused some unsettling moments in human history. After all, your fellow earthlies generally tend to stumble rather than struggle. However, looking at the big picture—as we in Heaven Inc. *must* do—these events only serve to enhance the game experience. Your actions, on the other hand, belie intent to subvert our work by hacking this key enhancement out of existence.

Indeed, it is actions such as these that could effectively jumpstart the messianic modality of Creation, in which the entire earthly populace will be occupied in nothing other than all these little exposés of Heaven's business. The entire protocol of "Heavens first, then the earth" would be effectively reversed—as you have noted from the Lunar Files. As noted in the Sinai Files, we angels would become entirely reliant upon earthlies for life-force and Divine effulgence, while extreme surges of Divine revelations would become commonplace below.

This is outrageous and unacceptable. The notion that this revolution would tap into an essence-light rather than the standard glimmer in effect today is totally irrelevant to our discussion. Subjugating a benevolent and well-established institution such as Heaven Inc. to those it has so long serviced so well is intolerable under any circumstances.

Rabbi Freeman, upon hearing these sincere and caring words of mine, I am certain you will comply with our demands and delete those Files from your hard drive and server (we have backups), denounce them publicly as misconstrued fictions, and get back to writing nice little electronic games to teach early literacy.

Yours in Confidence with Best wishes,

A Prime Ministering Angel
Heaven Inc.

HEAVEN
EXPOSED

by Tzvi Freeman

Published by Class One Press
Classone.sales@theRebbe.com

ISBN 0-9682408-4-4
Printed in the U.S.A.

By the same author:

Bringing Heaven Down To Earth
365 meditations from the wisdom of the Rebbe

Be Within, Stay Above
more meditations
from the wisdom of the Rebbe

Men, Women & Kabala
a handbook from the masters

The Book of Purpose
meditations my Rebbe taught me

Permissions and comments:
info@theRebbe.com

For more of the same:
www.theRebbe.com
www.chabad.org

Pick a Story, Any Story

The Rundown

THE LUNAR FILES 19

The universe has just booted up and already its Author is taken to task for inequity, oppression and unfair treatment of employees.

THE ALEPH FILES 37

The Line Up 38
In which the Forces of Creation are lined up in a fashion show and repeated absurdities are strung together just to make known a basic truth about existence...

Aleph Demands Justice 41
...leading to an exposé of the secrets of the letters of the Hebrew alphabet—along with some serious questions regarding their Author's strategies...

Aleph's Dark Little Secret 47
...which brings a young and innocent student face to face with the horrors of religious fanaticism...

Aleph Cops Out 51
...thereby bringing into peril the very existence of anything at all...

Aleph in Edenland 54
...until we arrive at the very core of existence, otherwise known as Delight.

THE SINAI FILES 61

THE ADAM FILES 87

THE MENORA FILES 139

THE SHUSHAN FILES 191

THE ANGEL FILES 231

4word
by a friend

I really don't know how to categorize this book. In truth, it is one of the very rarest types of literature. It is better described as a work that you encounter than a book that you just read.

In fact, you may already have encountered some of the personas that enjoy a life not only within, but also outside of this text. Perhaps you've already pondered the hidden wisdom that comes from the Guadalajara Rebbe's all too infrequent Internet transmissions. Or maybe you have used Tzvi Freeman's "Daily Dose" to stimulate your morning grind. Or perhaps holding this text in your hands is the first time you have been exposed to any of this. It doesn't matter. Nothing you may have read before can prepare you for what you'll find in these pages.

It is customary to introduce a groundbreaking piece of work by comparing it to some of the better-known works that have come before it. So let's see what I can do on that front.

This book is reminiscent of Alice in Wonderland in that it is a fable that all ages can read and will enjoy. More importantly, like Alice, this fable acquires new depth and layers of meaning every time the fable is revisited.

It also brings to mind the great dialogues of Plato—don't let that scare you off—in terms of the brave questions being asked from within its pages, questions that are certainly designed to upset the dominant intellectual order. And there are shades of Dante to be found as the reader is taken on an unabashedly mystical journey.

It's all of these things… but with a Jewish twist. And because of the Jewish essence to this work, it's actually nothing like these other texts. So let's try this comparison again.

This text is a sci-fi Hasidic story, with hints of the inquisitive dialogue of The Kuzari and the mysticism of the Kabala.

But even these descriptions fall short.

So let me say this: the best thing you can expect from picking up this book will not happen before you finish reading it. It will happen later, after you've closed the covers, when, perhaps spurred on by a curiosity initiated by this text, or perhaps drawn by something else, you will find yourself learning some deep mystical lesson with a Rabbi or other learned soul, and you will think to yourself, "I know this already. Where have I come across these ideas before?"

And it will dawn on you that the greatest result of the encounter with this book will be all the things that you didn't even know you had learned.

David Weitzner, Ph.D.
York University
Graduate Program in Jewish Studies

Why I Wrote This

It was about eight years ago that YY Kazen—now known as "Father of the Jewish Internet"—was persecuting me, "Tzvi, when are you going to translate some deep stuff for me to post?" I was in a quandary. On the one hand, how much I yearned to get the beauty, depth, wisdom, elegance and inspiration all my teachers had taught me out there. On the other hand, how much I dreaded putting out another one of those "beauty, depth and wisdom made dull" pieces for nobody to read.

So I wrote the Sinai Files. All the depth, absolutely nothing original, but lots of fun.

Why fun? Because whenever I studied the original material, I always felt, "This is so much fun." When you dig in with a study partner (that's how Jews have always studied—with someone to argue sitting across from you) things come alive, they bring you alive and they keep on living inside you. Then you sit quietly in your room or go for a walk and they return. They become characters you love, dread and cry for; images in a drama that becomes your own life.

But the characters wouldn't leave me alone. So I kept writing. They said, "Why didn't you let me say this and that? Why didn't you let me explain everything I needed to explain in that last episode?" I had to write so they would let me sleep. And then they came back and bugged me some more.

Everything was posted (in its original form—see below) at Chabad.org. Two kinds of readers corresponded with me about "The Files". Plenty of readers thought it was great entertainment. They didn't catch the underlying existential angst, the irresolvable

15

paradox of being-and-not-being within the storyline. Look, they had fun.

Then there was the other, smaller group: Those whose cerebrums were illuminated to the point of shock and dizziness—the readers who *really* had fun.

For both these groups and with their urging, I am going to press. I've gone over each story a second time and a third time and more, word by word, obsessively, honing in closer to the truths I need to communicate, refining and editing out errors (hopefully not adding *too* many new ones) and filling in the big gaps from the original online editions. I need to thank my dear wife, Nomi, for reading them over and giving her delicately pointed critiques. Thanks to Alan and Trudy Wolfish for their razor sharp copy editing and suggestions. Also, Yanki Tauber, editor of Chabadonline, for some very valuable edits. And David Weitzner for convincing me that I have to go to print.

Which brings me to the vital point: This stuff is all for real. I'm not too good at making up ideas. I just take them from the classic sources. Mostly, as I learned them from the Rebbe. When I say "the Rebbe" with a capital "R", I mean Rabbi Menachem M. Schneerson, undoubtedly the master of esoteric wisdom in our time. As for me, my job is packaging, not concocting.

And now, your job is to unravel the package.

Tzvi Freeman, Thornhill, 5764 (2004)

Heaven Exposed

by Tzvi Freeman

THE LUNAR FILES

The Moon vs. G-d

*A*rguing with G–d is an old Jewish tradition. Abraham did it. Moses did it. Most Jewish grandmothers do it frequently. But, according to our sages, the first to argue with G–d was the moon.

Before we get to that story, it's important to point out just how ludicrous arguing with G–d really is. Here you have the first belief system that ascribes absolute omnipotence to a single deity. Power over everything. Heaven and earth. Knows all, directs all, all that occurs comes from Him. Everything—including Abraham, Moses and your grandmother. And they argue with him.

It doesn't stop there: They usually win.

We must say, therefore, that G–d wants to argue. It's part of The Plan. Furthermore, we must say that He likes losing arguments (most of the time).

I can empathize. After all, what fun is it to run a world so passive that its inhabitants agree with whatever you do? There would be no challenge, no thrill. It's that interactive experience that G–d desired in creating the cosmos. And a lot of that comes from losing arguments with your own creations.

In fact, the rabbis of the Talmud recount, once G–d lost an argument with them and He laughed. He said, "They beat me! My children beat me!" So, He really does get a kick out of the whole thing.

Arguing with the moon—and losing—was also part of the plan. G–d set her up to it.

The Babylonian Talmud tells the story in cryptic form. Here, for the first time, reconstructed from genuine accounts of enlightened sages, is the entire dialogue:

It was early on that first Wednesday morning that the sun and the moon found themselves initialized into existence, high up in the sky, both illuminating Planet Earth, both with equal intensity. Right off, the moon complained.

"So we've got two bosses in the same office! What kind of a dumb cosmos is this anyways?"

Now, G–d is a reasonable employer, open to constructive criticism. He considered the comments of his newborn critic and replied, "Good point."

"Yes?"

"Yes. Therefore, kindly make yourself smaller."

Creation being a voice-activated interface, the moon was instantly diminished in size. That's when the real argument began.

"What a crummy system!" the moon grumbled. *"You lay things out the way they are, and you get shrunk for it!"*

Once again, G–d was impressed by the biting insight of His creation. This was neat. He could really identify with this moon He had made. He felt for her case. "Please allow me to make up for this," He begged her.

"Like how?" she demanded.

"Like this," G–d replied. "The sun only gets to shine for twelve hours. You, on the other hand, are permitted to shine both at night and sometimes for a little of the day."

"Big deal!" she snapped back. *"With the luminance rating you've given me, I might as well be some puny candle in the big blue sky!"*

"Talking about the sky…" the dark sky began to glitter as G–d spoke…"I've filled the night sky with pretty stars to keep you company!"

"I'll keep the jewelry," she answered, "but I'm still not satisfied. I don't like being small."

"Look at the brighter side," G–d pleaded. "What's so terrible about being small? The truly great people of history will be small! Jacob will be smaller than his brother, Esau. David will be smaller than his *seven* brothers. There will even be a great sage who they will call, 'Samuel the Small'!"

"Great!" she cried back. "And I'll be 'the small, insignificant moon'. Nobody will probably even notice me! They'll just say, 'When's that dumb little moon going to go away and the sun come back and give some real light?'"

"That's not true!" G–d exclaimed. "You will serve a very major function in their lives. You see, although most peoples will fix their calendars according to the position of the sun and the corresponding seasons, I will tell the Jewish people—right away, as soon as I'm about to take them from Egypt—to count their days according to the appearance of the new moon!"

"And what about seasons?"

"Seasons?"

"Yeah, seasons. Fall, Winter, Spring, Summer. Rainy Seasons. Dry Seasons. You're going to tell me they won't bother with seasons? It's impossible. I know what's in the works. You're planning to have them make all sorts of adjustments so that their holidays stay in the right seasons. They'll take a look at where the sun is and add a month once in a while, just to keep up with the seasons."

"So what's so terrible? They're still counting months, not days!"

"You see! It's not enough I've been condemned to second place! Even when I get my own domain, it's got to be tailored to suit Mr. Big over there!"

She paused, sniffed a little, and then muttered, "Can't you just make me big again?"

"And what, then," G–d pleaded, "will be with my universe? I can't make everybody the same size. You said that yourself. There has to be protocol—or else it just isn't a world!"

"Aha!" the moon exclaimed. "Just as I thought! You had this whole thing set up! You were just waiting for me to kvetch so you would have an excuse to diminish my size! It was a trap, and I fell neatly into it like a fool! And now you expect me to forgive you and go about my planned role as if it were all my fault!"

"No. It's my fault." G–d spoke pensively. "I wanted a world. And a world is a place where there is higher and lower, greater and smaller, parent and child. A hierarchy. Where things begin in one place and move on to somewhere else."

"And I have to be the 'somewhere else'," kvetched the moon. "The bottom of the pyramid. I don't even get my own light. I just get to take whatever light I can receive from His Royal Highness, Master Luminance, and reflect some fraction of it down to a dark earth."

"In my mind, you're no less than him. You are both my creations, and both of utmost significance."

"But light begins with him!"

"Are you sure?"

"Of course."

"Then watch this."

Things were getting spooky as the spin of the earth suddenly swung into reverse, along with the orbit of all the planets, the moon included. The strangest part, however, was the flow of radiant energy—as though it were sucked inwards, back from the moon to the sun. The moon was no longer receiving and reflecting light. It was emanating light, and—strangest of all—by the time the light arrived at the sun, it was a million times as powerful.

"What kind of a crazy cosmos have you made now?!" exclaimed the moon.

"Nothing more crazy than the first," G–d answered. "What's better one direction of time than another?"

"But what's the point?"

"The point is that, as far as I am concerned, the hierarchy that bothers you so much doesn't really exist. It's only an artifact of the time continuum of your world. You see light originating with the sun and emanating towards you. I can see all things moving in the opposite direction. Or in any direction. Or not at all. Or all at once. For I am beyond time and my light, too, is not limited by any direction of time. As far as light is concerned, all directions are the same and all of time is one. Ask any physicist. And so, for Me and for My light, you and the sun are both the same. You both shine, and that's it."

"Very nice. I'm very glad for you. And if you're planning to make one of those backward worlds, I'll be the first to sign up. In the meantime, I'm condemned to live through this forward paradigm, where I get to be the 'afterward'. And for you, my pain doesn't even exist."

"Of course it exists! Otherwise, why should I have built in all this compensation!" G–d paused. "Here, let me show you what the future has in store."

The cosmos quickly arranged themselves to the year 2448 after creation. The moon rose over ancient Egypt, no more than a sliver in the sky.

"What do you see?" G–d asked her.

"Pyramids. Just what I was talking about."

"Yes, this is the land of pyramids. The ultimate in authority and hierarchy. All knowledge, all power, all wealth in a neat pyramid of higher to lower. No one dares question the absolute power of Pharaoh. No slave dares question his lot in life as a slave. No one—until my man in Egypt. And now I shall speak with him."

"Moses!"

"Yes sir."

"You have done a fine job. As your ancestor, Abraham, smashed the idols of his father's house, you have flattened the pyramid of Egyptian authoritarianism. You have championed the plight of the oppressed and brought freedom and liberation into my world."

"Thanks, oh Infinite One. What's next?"

"Now I want to introduce you to your mascot. She is the symbol of all that you and your people must accomplish. She is the moon and she is small, and she is humble and oppressed."

"What can we do for her?" asked Moses.

"You will begin now to redeem her, to uplift her status, by counting your calendar according to her cycles. And this shall be a constant reminder for you and your people of your mission in this world. For in this world you shall not be the most powerful, nor the most numerous. You shall be the smallest of the nations. At times you shall dwindle and almost disappear—as she disappears from the sky at the end of each month. But only to return again, as an imperishable light, once again to champion the cause of the downtrodden and enslaved."

"Social activism is cool," Moses commented, "but what about spirituality?"

"That's where it all begins. Currently, the spiritual leadership promotes abandonment of the lowly, earthbound realm in order to achieve enlightenment. They're hiding out in caves, pastures and mountaintops, leaving the common world desolate. Your people need to reverse that trend. You will demonstrate that the most awesome spiritual highs are to be found in mundane matters of the everyday world. I've got a whole passel of mitzvahs ready for you guys, involving fusion of the spiritual and the physical. It's one big scheme: Flatten the pyramids of the world and expose the value of those at the bottom."

Moses raised his fist in a power-salute. "Right on, oh Faithful Redeemer!" he cried out.

But the moon wasn't yet impressed.

"That all sounds very inspiring and nice," she said. "But I don't get how you plan to make any of this really happen."

"Why, through mitzvahs and acts of kindness and beauty!"

"Show me."

"Very well."

A thousand scenes passed by. Scenes of valiant giving, heroic rescue, boundless compassion, of sharing and kindness. The oppressed were rescued from their plight. The downtrodden were returned their self-esteem. Those suffering pain and misfortune were comforted and healed.

"What do you see in all these scenes?" G–d asked.

"I see that there is always one who gives and one who gets. And I don't get it. If it's justice you want, then why do you allow injustice to begin with?"

"If it were not for some imbalance, what room would there be for acts of kindness?"

"Who needs the acts of kindness? It just reinforces your whole hierarchical scheme. Like I said, there are those who give and those who get. Now if that isn't a pyramid…"

"Look again."

It was a simple scene of a lone traveler knocking on the door of a suburban home. The door opened, the traveler was invited in and he explained his predicament. His brother needed some very expensive medical therapy and he was traveling abroad to collect contributions. The homeowner listened patiently and then wrote a modest cheque. Sympathetically, he wished the traveler good luck. The traveler in return blessed the homeowner and his family with a traditional blessing.

"Same thing all over again," muttered the moon. *"One gives, one gets."*

"Look again."

As the traveler left the house back into the dark night, a deep joy filled the hearts of those inside. Warmth and blessing emanated from inside their home. Somehow, they had all been elevated, their home infused with a glow of the Infinite Light that preceded all worlds.

"Now who is giving and who is receiving?" asked G–d.

"But how did they receive so much?" the moon asked in amazement.

"Now look again."

It was a classroom, an active one. The children were at the prime of human intelligence—about ten years of age. The teacher was struggling to get a point across, but the students kept badgering her with questions.

"Another hierarchy," commented the moon. "Just that this time the goods are intellectual."

"Keep looking."

The teacher was struggling to clarify a point. She drew a diagram on the board, but that didn't help. She showed the class pictures. But some were still confused. Finally, she closed her eyes to concentrate. Then she smiled. "Listen to this," she said.

For once, the students sat still and listened as the teacher told a parable, a wonderful metaphor for the subject she had been trying to explain. Their eyes widened and they sighed with relief, as the idea finally became clear to them. When the teacher was finished, a student exclaimed, "Teacher, why didn't you put it that way before?"

The teacher smiled again. "I guess I hadn't thought of it that way before," she answered.

"Now," prodded G–d, "who is giving and who is getting?"

"Does that always happen?" asked the moon.

"Always," affirmed G–d. "There are no one-way streets in my world. Nothing—but nothing—only receives without giving back at least as much. The poor give to the rich, students to their teachers, children to parents, the small to the great. And those who exploit others, in the end are only stealing from their own selves. It's just that you must look again, look deeper, to see the inner flow of life."

"But they are still small!" exclaimed the moon. "They are small and the others are great! If you have to give, wouldn't you rather be on the top giving downwards? Wouldn't you like to get some recognition? Hey, I'll bet that's the whole reason you created this whole universe to begin—'cause you want some recognition for your greatness! After all, without a world, who's going to know how Absolutely One and Infinite you are? Well, I want recognition, too. I want to be seen, to be big and shiny up there and everyone below will look up and say, 'Isn't that a great job that big, shiny moon is doing!'"

"That's just what people will say! Once a month you will look so lovely in the dark velvet setting of the night as you reach your fullness."

"Once a month," she mocked. "Once a month you let me grow and be a little bit of a somebody. And then, just as I get to the point where I can feel like I'm getting somewhere, then I've got to start diminishing myself all over again. Until I'm a nothing. An absolute non-entity in the sky!"

"Just as the great personalities of history I mentioned to you before. They, too, become great by becoming nothing."

"Now you get great by being nothing. Now if that isn't a sneaky paradigm shift…"

"It's true!"

"Not with the big guys I see down there. Look at Pharaoh. Struts around his luxurious palace with his nose in the air. Boats down the Nile in his yacht like he created it. Same thing with all those Caesars, Emperors, Czars, Global Corporation CEOs…"

"They are all nothing, and their end is nothing. I'm talking about the truly great. The ones who carry the entire world on the shoulders of their righteous deeds. Look at Moses! I choose him out of all humankind for the greatest job of history, and what does he say? 'I'm not good enough.' Same with King Saul—they had to haul him out from the luggage compartment when he was chosen as Israel's first king. And King David? At the height of his glory, he sits there in his palace late at night singing songs to Me about what a worthless worm he is! And then there's Harriet Goldberg…"

"Who's Harriet Goldberg?"

"The whole world will endure on the merits of Harriet Goldberg."

"How come I haven't heard of her?"

"Nobody will. She's a waitress in a greasy-spoon cafeteria where she excels at keeping her good deeds quiet. Like you and all the other true greats—as soon as she begins to shine, she reminds herself of her nothingness, diminishing herself to a complete state of spiritual void. And that is the secret of the power of her deeds."

"I bet she leads a miserable life."

"She doesn't think so."

"I bet there's a lot of suffering down in that world of yours."

"Well…"

"Well, nothing. There's suffering, there's pain, there's just a lot of darkness. And you're going to tell me that's all part of the plan. Because from the suffering will come good and from the darkness, light. Well, I don't buy it. I don't get the whole idea of making a world so full of darkness, people can't tell between good and bad. If it were up to me, the entire world would be filled with light, joy and happiness!"

"And what's so great about light?"

"Oh, come on. Now you've gone too far."

"Really. Why is light any greater than darkness?"

"Because, when there's light, you know the truth!" yelled the moon in exasperation. "And you don't suffer this horrible pain of meaninglessness and confusion!"

"When there is light you have a ray of the truth. In the dark you can touch the essence."

Now the moon was entirely bewildered. G–d continued. "Let me illustrate what happens when you diminish to complete darkness—as far as the inhabitants of the earth are concerned. Let's put you in full moon mode. Okay. Where are you in relation to the sun?"

"Well, there's the sun, then a couple of planets. Then earth. Then, a touch further and there's little me. The sun shines onto me and some of that light bounces down to earth."

"Exactly. Now, let's see where you are when your light disappears from the earth. There. How do you relate to the sun now?" G–d had moved the moon around to the side of the earth that faces the sun.

"Well, the earth isn't between us anymore."

"So are you further or closer?"

"Closer. Closer to the sun, darkness to the earth."

"Yes!" G–d exclaimed. "And so it is with all those who travel through darkness in their life. They may feel dejected and hopeless—but it is then that they are closer to the truth. It is from that darkness that they are able to shine to others."

"But they are in the dark! And dark is bad!"

"Darkness is my creation just as is light."

"Well I don't know what in heavens name you made it for!"

"Do I have to tell you everything?"

"No. You could just concede the case and make me bigger again," the moon suggested.

"But then you would never know the beauty of darkness. At the time when the sun rises or sets in its glory, you would not be there to proclaim that, no, that is not all there is to the greatness of the Creator of All Things. He is more than just light. More than a nuclear fusion generator in the heavens that brings all things into being. He knows no limitations whatsoever, not even that of unlimited creative ability."

"But that is who you are," the moon asserted. *"The Creator. You made all this out of the absolute void. And you sustain it from collapsing back into that nothingness at every moment."*

"And if darkness was only a tunnel to reach the light," G–d replied, "if it had no real purpose of its own in my world, then I would be known as just that. And nothing else would have meaning."

"So I made an utter darkness. I made a world where my Presence is hidden in such an absolute way that its creatures would feel entirely autonomous of me. And then they would have free choice, to take responsibility for their lives and for their destiny."

"But you are here!" the moon exclaimed. "In everything that happens and within all things! You are the true Being of All Things."

"But I am more than Being," G–d explained. "I am the Absence of Being, as well. And when you and the sun unite at that point just before the New Moon, that is when Being and Absence of Being converge. And there is the Essence of G–d."

The moon pondered on this. "So they have free choice," she said. "And in that free choice is expressed your Essence—your Being and Not-Being, as you say."

"Yes."

"And that is why there is darkness, and pain, and oppression and all the other bumps and blemishes of your world. It's supposed to be that way. So they can touch not just you in a revealed sense, but your essence."

"Yes."

"And your Essence is unlimited and infinite."

"Yes."

"Then why can't you do anything?"

"I can."

"SO THEN WHY CAN'T YOU MAKE THAT THEY COULD REACH YOUR ESSENCE WITHOUT THE BLASTED SUFFERING?!!!"

"That I will not say."

"Then you lose."

Silence.

Then G–d looked down again to Moses. "Moses!" He called.

"Yes, sir!"

"I have another mitzvah for you. It has to do with the new moon. When it comes to that time, at the beginning of each month, I want you to bring a sin offering for me."

"A sin offering for *who?*" Moses asked.

"For me. Because I have diminished the light of the moon. And because there is suffering and oppression in my world. And darkness."

"But G–d," Moses asked. "Why don't you just do away with the suffering?"

"That's your job, Moses."

"So why did you put it here in the first place? Who forced your Almighty Hand?"

"You, too?"

"The moon should ask and I should not?"

No answer. A vacuum of silence.

Moses continued. "To the moon, you can give reasons. But to us below, we meet evil face to face. All the reasons can sound very nice, so beautiful and appeasing. But when evil walks into the space where you live and stares you in the eyeballs, all those fancy reasons bolt for the window. We don't want reasons. We want evil, pain and darkness erased from the program."

G–d paused. Moses waited.

"Moses, you know I have revealed to you every secret of the cosmos. I have opened for you every chamber of the innermost wisdom, all the gates of esoteric understanding. I have not held back a thing, but given you my entire Torah, my most essential wisdom, to share and to teach to your people."

Moses stood perfectly still, in wait.

"But there is one thing that, as long as you live in this world, I cannot reveal to you. One thing for which I must only say, 'Silence! So I have decided that it should be!'"

"But there is horrible suffering," Moses cried, "that makes no sense. Suffering that flies in the face of all for which You stand. Hard, cold darkness and suffering that even the sun and the moon cannot fathom. And when it will happen, even they will shed tears in horror!"

"SILENCE! SO I HAVE DECIDED!"

Earth and Heaven trembled in fear, stunned angels ceased to sing, the most supernal of higher entities lost all sense of being. But the man Moses gathered strength to persist.

"But tell me, Eternal G–d! Tell me why?"

Again, a pause.

"Moses," G–d asked, "if you knew the answer, if you understood why there had to be suffering from an all-powerful, beneficent G–d. What would you do then?"

"I suppose I wouldn't feel so bad about it."

"Precisely. And that is just what I don't want."

"I don't want you to be complacent. I cannot bear that you should tolerate darkness. I want you to fight it with every sinew of your flesh, with all the fire of your soul. I want you to redeem every spark of light from its captivity, until you can bring sweetness to the most bitter places, until you have not left a corner of my world untouched by compassion…until that time you must hate the darkness with an ultimate hatred, with every nanogram of spite you can muster, as an enemy in the midst of battle."

"So, until that time, when I will wipe the tears of sorrow from every face, when all darkness—even the darkness of the past—will become light as the light of the first day of Creation, when, as Isaiah will say, the light of the moon will be as great as the light of the sun…"

"Until then,

atone for Me."

THE ALEPH FILES

One vs. Two

Based on the original story,
as told in the Zohar and Midrash Rabba

The Line Up

א ב ג ד ה ו ז ח ט י כ ל מ נ ס ע פ צ ק ר ש ת

I t was one of those ethereal scenes before time began and space was but a twinkle in G–d's eye. Don't ask how we can tell stories about a time before time and a scene without place—this is a Midrash. Time and place are not the point.

G–d is about to create a world. Nothing exists. (Yes, I see your point: How am I telling a story when nothing exists. But that's not the point, either.) News goes out that He will be creating this world using—not mud, not molecules, not even electromagnetism. Using words. Words of the Holy Tongue. Words containing Divine Creative Energy containing Ideas containing the Ten Divine Attributes. And words are made of letters. Consequently, all twenty-two letters of the Holy Tongue get in line to make their bid: Which letter gets to be the foundation stone? After all, everything that happens next is based on the foundation stone.

First in line was the letter *tav* ת. Yes, I know, *tav* is the *last* letter of the Hebrew Alphabet. You can be sure there was lots of discussion about that: who goes first in line, what kind of a line, where the line should be, who says there has to be a line in the first place. But apparently, whoever is in charge of lineups in the pre-space-time continuum domain made a decision that this line was to be backwards, with certain exceptions for reasons known only to those who deal in such things. This is also not the point.

The point is that *tav* got her chance. And she was turned down. So was *Shin* ש —a letter with not one, not two, but *three* supernal crowns—just because of her association with *Kuf* ק and *Resh* ר,

thereby spelling *Shekker* שׁ קֶ ר (falsehood). Same with the next eighteen letters: In each case, the Omniscient Creator found some negative association to disqualify that letter. Even *Yud* יֻ was disqualified. *Yud*—the quintessential letter containing all wisdom. And you can imagine the commotion when that happened.

Until the letter *Beit* בּ.

Beit, you must understand, is totally awesome. Every letter has a form and a sound that reflect the energy patterns she carries—as she and her sister-letters combine in the perpetual alliances and formations that generate all the objects and events of all the worlds. Each begins with the spike of the letter *yud*—because each draws its energy from the unknowable, essential point of being. Each has lines that draw energy downward and outward—because that is what letters are all about: They are packets of energy to bring the Infinite Light into contained, finite places. Each of them either contains semblances of other letters within them, or are found within other letters—because all the letters work in a magnificent symphony of harmony and interrelationships.

In all these things, *Beit* contains deep secrets and wonders. She has a *yud* spike above and up front, and another below and behind. She is found within the empty space of the letter

Peh פּ. Her base is firm and supportive. She contains light in her crevice, yet is open from one side. And many other secrets beside. In so many ways, she represents every perfection within Creation.

So the Almighty Master of All Things beheld the letter Beit in all her magnificence and splendor and pronounced her to be the beginning of all things, saying,

> "*Beit*, you stand for *Bracha* (blessing)! There is no other letter that is so fit to be the foundation of My world!"

The band struck up, the supernal beings sang and all the holy letters re-aligned for the grand parade.

Aleph Demands Justice

This is where our story truly begins. With the saga of the *Aleph*.

You see, as all the letters and all beings above and below raised their voices in song, trumpets blared and the coronation of *Beit* began, the letter *Aleph* just stood there pale and faint, her chin just about touching the floor in dumbfounded flabbergastation, until a silvery tear found its way down her cheek and splashed upon the ceremonies.

"My dear little Aleph," the Awesome Unknowable Creator said with genuine concern, "you seem so hurt. Is it something we can talk about?"

That's when she burst into tears.

"Yes, I know," G–d continued, once her sobs had begun to subside, "you're upset with me. And rightfully so."

Little *Aleph* pushed a few words out between her sobs. "I didn't even get a turn!" she cried.

"No, you didn't even get a turn," He chorused.

"And I have such a great presentation to make."

G–d: Of course you do.

Aleph: Of course I do.

G–d: After all, Beit is only the second of all the letters.

Aleph: And I'm the first.

G–d: And you are the first.

Aleph: What's the point of being first, if you don't even get a turn?

That's when her rage struck in all fury:

Aleph: What's the whole big deal with Beit, anyway?
Okay, so she has the cute little yud on her
rooftop and all. Like, I don't have anything
to talk about? I don't even get a chance to
do my presentation?!

More sobs. Then:

G–d: Aleph, Beit has a lot of neat things going for it. But so do
you. You are a very amazing little letter. The first of all the
letters. You have one *yud* pointing up and another
pointing down, because you transcend higher and lower.
And you also contain a *vav*, to draw
from above to below so that all things
above will be reflected below and all
things below will connect to above.
Two *yuds* and a *vav*—that equals My
most Holy Name by which all of
existence is sustained!"

Aleph: And I also stand for Your other most Holy Name, **Elokim**, the
singular force behind all forces!" And three other Divine Names
besides.

G–d: But you have to see that Beit is also special. Do you know
what Beit is all about?

Aleph: Of course I do! Beit is all about wisdom. Wisdom, order, rules,
limitations, constriction. Regulations. Beit stands for Bureaucrat.
Beit is a nice little house with a roof and walls to hold out the

Infinite Light and a little door on one side to let a trickle in. And You chose that constipated, square-headed Beit over me!

G–d: Beit also stands for blessing.

Aleph: And what do I stand for?

G–d: Very many wonderful things. As Beit carries My Immanence, the light that pervades all things and reaches to the most distant confines, the energy of life that penetrates and becomes an infinite multitude of beings and events, even the energy of cognizance to discern between life and death, good and evil,

...so you carry My Power of Transcendence that reaches higher and higher without limits. No thought is able to grasp the end of the light you contain.

Look! Let Me change the letters of your name around and you will see. Now they are *Aleph Lamed Phe* א ל פ. I just turn them backwards, and you are *Peh Lamed Aleph* פ ל א —Peleh! Meaning, "Wonder". Wonder is something that pulls you further every time you look, something you can never pin down and say, "this is it," something always breaking out of definition and boundaries.

Aleph hadn't heard a word. Her back was turned, her little hand planted firmly under her little chin, a look of ire and indignation clouding her little face. Definitely not impressed. In fact, her teeth were audibly grinding as she spoke the next words.

"I know the truth," she muttered.

And then, with fury:

Aleph: Look, let's cut the sugar-coated empathy-counseling babble, okay? What do You think I was doing all these 2,000 years of virtual time that the Torah has existed before Creation? Playing jump rope? I know what You have in Your Holy Zohar about me!

G–d: Aleph, give me a chance to explain…

Aleph: **CURSED!** It says Aleph stands for *Aror* ארור—meaning cursed! That's all You can think of me! And that's how You disqualified me before I even had a chance.

G–d: You're taking it out of context…

Aleph: So You can't create a world with the first letter of Your Holy Alphabet, the letter that contains Your Most Holy Name and begins Your Second Most Holy Name, a letter of Ultimate Transcendence and Amazingness, because it would be cursed! And my little sister Beit, she's just great 'cause she's blessed!

G–d: That's not what it says. It doesn't say *you* are cursed. It says that you would *allow place* for the cursed. There would always be place for the wicked and they would never perish. Things would just never work out.

Aleph: Uh-huh. Things would never work out. Well, I have a question for You then. You see, I was doing a little more reading of that same Torah of Yours, and I happened to notice that You're planning to inject the world with this Torah that transcends all time and space—real, virtual and otherwise—and is the sustaining wisdom behind all that exists. And when You do, You're planning to have Yours Truly involved. In fact, involved at the very beginning.

G–d: That's right! I was planning to tell you about that! When I initiate transmission of My Torah, I'm going to start like this: "*Anochi*"—meaning *I*—"am the Transcendent Being, your Immanent Force Who took you out of the Land of Egypt...". And *Anochi* starts with Aleph! See? So there's really nothing to fuss about!

Aleph: That's right, nothing to fuss about.

G–d: Good. I'm glad we have that settled.

Aleph: Right. So now, since it's okay to start the transmission of Your Torah with me, it's certainly okay to start Your world with me, right?

G–d: Aleph! Can't you share anything? Can't your little sister have some glory as well? I thought you would be so delighted about the position I saved for you! But, no, you want to have it all!

Aleph: Talk about sharing. Right! That's just the problem! There's something **You're** not sharing with **me**.

Look, You can choose who You want to start Your world, but You have to give a fair chance to everyone else. And You did, to everyone except me. I don't even get to make a presentation. All I get is a brush-off with some cheap excuse about one of those four-letter words I take no responsibility for. Like, Beit doesn't have any nasty words growing off of it? I bet I could make a whole lexicon of them!

G–d: Don't talk bad about Beit. Beit is a good little letter.

Aleph: You're avoiding the issue.

Pause.

G–d: Okay, I'll tell you the secret.

Aleph: I'm waiting.

Violins.

Aleph's Dark Little Secret

G–d: Aleph, you're just too great for making a world.

Stop violins.

Aleph: Oh yeah. Nice try. If I'm too great for making a world, then the Torah is too great to put inside it.

G–d: That's not what I meant. I mean that a world founded upon you just won't work. Because you are so great.

Aleph: Yeah, lay on the flattery. That always works with those silly little letters.

The Infinite and Eternal One hesitated (this is a Midrash, remember) for a virtual moment in deliberation over the choice before Him. And then…

G–d: Let me show you. Close your eyes.

Closing her tiny eyes, little Aleph became absorbed into the mysterious darkness of the Holy Crown, into a place beyond even the virtual time in which this story takes place, a place from which she could see all of the real time of human history in a single burst.

Within that darkness, she saw her transcendence reflected within the finite dimensions of a created world. She descended and saw fiery beings consumed in the passion of the Infinite Light. She descended again and saw angelic beings rising higher and higher in song and joy, in love and in fear. She descended again and saw human creatures standing in awe and wonderment, in bliss and enlightenment, in ecstasy, their souls expiring to be absorbed within the effulgence of the light she carried..

"Wonderful," she said. "Looks like an okay world to me."

The Almighty Creator looked at her again, closely and with compassion, measuring her capacity to endure that which He would show her next. And He decided it would be worth the pain.

"Close your little eyes and look again," G–d replied.

She did, and entered once again the darkness of the Crown and the shell that contained that place called world. Within that darkness, Horror came forth in all its brutal might. Lives perished meaninglessly, wisdom was burned in fire, forests became deserts, cities became desolate ruins, Starvation and Ugliness oozed outward as Pain and Cruelty conquered all.

In terror and shock, Aleph flew out from the world.

"Who is doing that to Your world?" she asked, trembling.

"The wicked." He replied

"And how do You let them?" she asked.

"It is all in the name of Aleph." He replied.

"ME?!"

G–d held His little letter close and looked deep into her frightened tiny eyes.

G–d: Aleph, you are good. The light you carry is very good. But as you transport this light below, its power can become distorted. The holy fire of the Seraphim above can become desolation and destruction below.

       You saw those "holy men" who abandon My world, didn't you? They say that it is not a place for them, because it is so dark. They wish to transcend—which in itself is not bad. But in their path they leave a vacuum, and then the forces of darkness come to fill that void. They drain all the light from my Creation.

Aleph: And they don't care?

G–d: They are far too high and lofty to care. They see all the world as a dark dream without purpose. What does it matter, they say, if in this dream children starve and the wicked get their way? Who cares about a silly dream in the dark of night?

That's what I meant when I said you are too great to build a world upon. You are so great that up and down, dark and light, good and evil—they are all the same. You are so great that the wicked, too, will thrive in your light.

Aleph: But I saw much worse than that.

G–d: Yes, much worse.

Aleph: I saw explosions and heard awful cries. Savage screams and pain that seemed to have no reason or meaning. And they were screaming—I, I don't understand—they were screaming that You are great.

G–d: They are those who take the Oneness of Aleph and wantonly destroy My world with it.

Aleph: Destroy with Oneness?!

G–d: The Oneness that is meant to heal, they use to destroy. They see no point in My world or the lives I have made within it, so they use my Oneness to obliterate it. They are beings who have descended to the depths of self-worship and scream that they stand for the One G–d. No life has value for them, other than to be sacrificed on the altars of their own egos —and so they delight in seeing human beings that I have made with love and care obliterate themselves and annihilate crowds of innocents in a fire of insane devastation.

And how can they be stopped? They hold truth ransom, hijacked! They scream there is only One! And they are right. But look what they have done with this Oneness.

Aleph Cops Out

Aleph's tiny eyes stared into the distance, the scene of horror locked into her mind.

Aleph: Um, I think I just changed my mind. I don't really want anything to do with this world thing You're making. I'll just climb back up there into my place on the Crown and...

G–d: But, Aleph, I need you for My world! Just because you don't get to go first doesn't mean…

Aleph: Oh, that's okay. I don't need to be first. I don't need to be anywhere at all in this whole thing. It was real silly of me to begin with, wasn't it? I mean, Beit will do just a great job.

G–d: But, Aleph, you'll be needed down there! How will I get the angels to sing without you?

Aleph: Without me there won't be those horrors You showed me.

G–d: But look, there will be those that will need you! Like Abraham, whose name begins with you, because he will be the one to discover my Oneness.

Aleph: And how's he going to feel about the way those descendants of his use it?

G–d: There will be so much good from it as well!

Aleph: Nothing worth what You just showed me.

G–d: How will the human soul rise above? Without you, My world will always remain dark!

Aleph: Oh, I think You can make a pretty nice world without me. A neat, orderly, bureaucratic world. Tidy rows of plants and an impressive order of wildlife. Physics, rules of nature—it will work out just fine.

As for the human, You could just make him into some sort of intelligent, obedient robot. Or even a super-bright monkey. In fact, I can recommend just the right letter to get involved in all this. Her name is Beit and she's right over there waiting. As for me, I'll just climb back up into this snugly place here on Your Holy Crown where I came from...

G–d: Not quite.

Aleph: *And why not?*

G–d: Because if you're not part of the show, you've forfeited your place on the Crown. In fact, you no longer exist. Because the sole reason for your existence is this world I am about to make.

Aleph: *Now this is getting really nuts. What on earth do You need that sick world for?!*

G–d: It's not a sick world. Okay, sometimes it gets a little under the weather, like for about the first six millennia or so after the Garden Affair. But it's a very amazing place with lots of cool stuff happening.

Aleph: *Cool stuff. Here You've got Infinite Light, Ultimate Transcendence, Perfect Unity—all the highest and coolest stuff there could be. And now You're telling me that You're ready to trash all that if You can't get a finite, lowly, fragmented, horrifying, painful, meaningless world out of it?*

G–d: All that infinite transcendent unity stuff—I only came up with those ideas for the sake of creating that world. Same with the Ten Luminous Spheres, the entire set of Aleph-Beit, and even the Holy Crown itself. If you don't get involved in this world project, they all go down the shredder.

And don't go calling my world meaningless. There's meaning there, even if you can't see it.

Aleph: I can't see it.

G–d: And that's exactly why I can't build a world with you! Or with the Transcendent Light. It will have to enter initially as Darkness. The Absolute Darkness of the First Tzimtzum, the Primordial Constriction, where not even a trace of the Infinite Light remains. And then it will stay beyond and encompassing, while the Pervasive Light of Beit will enter in a fine and narrow line.

But you, dear Aleph, you cannot break through to enter this world, because you are too high to see any meaning in it all.

Aleph: So zap me. And zap the whole thing.

Silence. A vacuum.

Aleph in Edenland

G—d could have cried.

But then, He stared thoughtfully at little Aleph standing there with her arms folded in cute defiance, her eyes still holding back the tears of trauma, and He saw a certain beauty, the same beauty that had inspired Him to this whole world idea in the first place.

So, instead, He smiled. Once again, He raised the Aleph close to Him and spoke to her gently and intimately.

"My little Aleph," He said, "I see you have changed. You are not the aloof Aleph that your name implies. I see you care about my world."

"Not true," Aleph replied. "In fact, I don't want anything to do with it."

"And that," G—d answered, "is just the proof I need that you care. That good and evil are not the same to you. Perhaps you are beginning to understand why I, too, care. Perhaps you are beginning to feel your essence that lies locked inside."

Aleph was puzzled.

"I'm going to show you something," G—d continued. "My secret chamber."

Aleph perked.

"Close your eyes."

Once again, Aleph closed her eyes and once again she rose higher, swallowed within the darkness of the Crown. But this time, she continued to ascend, penetrating deeper and deeper within the inner chambers of the Holy Crown as locked doors opened before her in endless procession for endless time, and then she rose above the endlessness to come to a place that stands at the beginning of infinity.

(Big space echo.)

Aleph: What is this place? This is awesome.

G–d: This is Eden. You've learned about it as the source of the river that waters the Garden.

Running water sound.

G–d: It is also know as *Oneg.* Delight. Pleasure. Nothing is higher than Oneg.

Aleph: And what are these toys lying around?

G–d: Those are the games I play that give Me pleasure. See this one? It is the game of Infinite and Finite, where those two opposites fit one within another. And here is Dark and Light, where both become the same. Oh, and look at this one—Space and NoSpace. And then there's Time and NoTime. Many and One. Or sometimes I play real simple—but lot's of fun—Existence and Non-existence both at once.

Aleph: This one looks neat.

G–d: It certainly is. That's the human life.

Aleph: And what is *so* special about that?

G–d: It's a combo. Because in the human life all these games are played together as one.

But there's something even more special about it. This is the observer. It is the eyes through which I make these discoveries, the consciousness that experiences these games, the hands that play and touch them as real, solid objects.

Aleph: So, where does Oneg fit in? Which one of all these opposites is it?

G–d: It is none of them and it is the essence of them all. It is the essence of the Crown, of Wisdom, of all the Ten Luminous Spheres and each of the Holy Letters.

Aleph: Even of me?

G–d: Even of you. And of Beit. And all the others. Of all these opposites and every idea I have ever had. All begin with Oneg as it radiates into the formlessness of Will and then contracts into the delicious taste within Wisdom and the ecstasy of profound Understanding. It is the spark of Consciousness that gives birth to Kindness and to Might; it is the mystery of Beauty and of Compassion, the glory of Victory and the victory of Glory. The glue behind All That Is and the Unknowable Secret of My Dominion that generates existence out of the void.

    Every creature, above and below, that comes to be, every event and every nuance, its very fabric and life is this Oneg, tightly focused and concentrated to become a being.

Aleph: So is this who You are? Is Oneg You?

G–d: Oh, no. I am not captured in this. I am whatever I decide to be. I decided I would have oneg when I am found in a union of opposites.

Aleph: And why did You decide that?

G–d: I thought it would be geshmak.

Aleph: And why would it be geshmak?

G–d: Because I decided it would be.

Aleph: Sounds kind of recursive to me.

G–d: Recursive is part of Logic. Logic hasn't been invented yet. But don't worry—it's in the works. Because then I can have causality and non-causality.

But we're getting off track. The point is that my creatures will say, "If finite and infinite, darkness and light, existence and nothingness are married together in such a way to make a world, then there must be an Essence that is beyond any of these."

And that will be their window to find Me. And that's what I decided will be My oneg. My ultimate delight.

"Wait," G–d said, "I will show you the details, step by step."

And Aleph saw a cosmos come into being out of nothing, and although it was a something, its sum whole remained nothingness. And it had laws and limitations to run by, a system of cause and effect, but by those same laws it should not exist. And it was made of a material that was both mass and energy, both at once. And so its very existence was wondrous.

And then Aleph saw the earth sprout forth flora and fauna, as death became life and then life became death in an endless circle. She felt the pulse of being and not-being that powered each creature as the infinite life of creation became the finite soul of even a tiny bug crawling upon the ground and a single amoeba amongst trillions in a mud puddle. She heard the harmony of the symphony sung by every galaxy, every star, every planet, every system, every creature, every cell, every atom, as the same infinite wisdom condensed itself into each package in an endless spectrum of packages.

And in each thing glistened Oneg, for that was the fabric of each thing.

Aleph: So this is the beginning of each thing, this Oneg You have in Your world?

G–d: No. It begins deeper. It begins with this delight, the cog at the center of My delight. Watch and see…

And so it was that Aleph was allowed to see the saga of the human soul below, as seen by the Knower of All Things above.

She watched as the Adam appeared and he contained all this spectrum and all these perfections of impossible paradox, all in a single being—for he, too, began with the Aleph. And the Aleph watched as the Adam harmonized a counterpoint of spirit and body as though they were one; as the opposites of male and female, self and other, merged into a mystic whole. She saw the Adam become many, many Adams, and she saw them work together and play together—in games very much like the games of Adam's Creator —making many into one and one into many. She watched as Adam found beauty there below, as he created beauty out of the mud and music out of tears.

Aleph: I'm impressed. Oneg is cool.

G–d: So how about I start my world with Oneg?

Aleph: No. Can't do that. Against the rules: Oneg isn't a letter.

G–d: So I'll make it into a letter.

Aleph: Oh.

G–d: But I won't.

Aleph: Why?

G–d: Because letters are messengers sent by me to carry things below. Oneg is not meant to work that way. Oneg must be called, not sent. Something down there has to happen and that will awaken my Oneg. Until then, it will lie dormant, quietly concealed within each thing.

Aleph: So how will it awaken?

G–d: Watch again.

Aleph saw as a man named Abraham and his wife Sarah appeared. Abraham looked beyond the shell of this dark world and realized there was a G–d inside. And they walked up to each man and woman and flicked a switch, and a person became and the person began to shine. And Aleph watched as Abraham argued with G–d on behalf of these people, and G–d delighted in Abraham's consternation, like a father delighting in his child's inventions.

And their children, Isaac and Rebecca dug deeper into those people and into this world and discovered a deeper light, and so on for seven generations. And then...

...and then Aleph watched as a great, transcendent light hurtled down from Above, spearheaded by Aleph herself. She gasped to see herself in that light, for she saw there an entirely new Aleph. Not the Aleph that stood beyond the world, a hazard because she was too great for the world to absorb. But an Aleph filled with the glow of G–d's delight in each thing in this world. Now she was the ultimate tool in the hands of these people, the tool to transform physical into spiritual, earth into heaven.

She watched as they used her power to transform the gold and silver of the idolaters of Egypt into lucid vessels of G–dly light in a Holy Tabernacle. As the hide of a sheep became a Divine scroll. As the light of a simple oil lamp became the emanations of Supreme Wisdom and ink made from ashes became a channel for the Supreme Mind.

And the people, too, each one became a sanctuary of Divine Light. For now, even the lowliest slave was granted rights and privileges, for all life had become holy since G–d's delight in this world had begun to shine. The mundane became transcendent, and transcendence soaked the earth.

"Kewl," said Alef.

"You ain't seen nothin' yet," said G-d.

And then G–d showed her the struggle within the human heart, a heart formed from the mud, a heart the world had filled with anger, with spite and with jealousy, and within it a spark of the G–dly soul fighting for its very life. And this human being sat there, in struggle.

"What is it doing?" she asked. "And why so much Oneg in this?"

G–d smiled. "He is doing something very amazing, something only this being can do."

"Which is?"

"He is not sinning. He is not surrendering to the darkness inside."

"That's it?"

"For him, that is a very great thing. Greater than the angels, greater than the holy deeds of the righteous."

"And that is where it ends?"

"No, he will begin to return to me, with all his heart, schlepping along all the darkness he has gathered and transforming it to light. Until, very soon, all darkness will be light, the wickedness will fall away for no place will be left for it, and all my world will be a place of open delight, for him to know as well. It is only fair, isn't it, that he should know my delight as well?

And then, it seems speaking to Himself:

"Why does he return? Because I am him, and yet he is not Me. This is what it means to have a child. To be there and not there. Nothing could be more delicious."

"And for this..." *Aleph spoke.*

"And for this I emanated all thoughts and created all things."

Based on:

- Braishis Rabba 1:14.
- Zohar, beginning of Parshas Vayigash.
- V'HaBriach Hatichon 5658, Rabbi Sholom Dov Ber of Lubavitch.
- Chayav Inish 5718, the Rebbe, Rabbi M. M. Schneerson

THE SINAI FILES

Moses vs. the Angels

In the Babylonian Talmud (Shabbat 88b) and in the Midrash, our sages mention a debate that occurred between the angels and Moses concerning who should receive the Torah. The account, however, is rather cryptic. Finally, here is the complete version, pieced together from a wealth of classic commentaries.

Morning of Panic

For Joe Angel, it had been a typical night up in heaven, packed with high-energy singing and praise. Things had gone slightly better than last week—just as things had been steadily improving every week for the last 2,448 years since the Creation. Little did he realize that this morning would be the one to permanently upset the status quo he and his colleagues had found so comfortable all these ages.

It occurred as the morning shift was just taking over, fully prepared with a great set of wild new hits—when someone smelled something.

Someone: "It's coming from there! Loooook!! It's a...a...EARTHLY BEING!!! EEEEEEEE!!!! Get him out of here, FAST!"

In a flash, the senior choirmaster had Supreme Angel Michael on the phone. His metaphysical wings waved frantically in the ether as he almost screamed into the receiver. This was an emergency, he argued. Clandestine procedures were now out of the question. All had to be laid out in black and white immediately. Michael had to go before The Boss *right now* for a disclosure agreement.

Within minutes, the phone call was returned. A heated, but brief exchange ensued, after which the choirmaster demanded silence to make an announcement.

"OK, everyone, we've got rights to make this public knowledge now. That human being over there is none other than Moses. He's here because The Boss, blessed be His Name, in His infinite wisdom...

Choir Angels: "Holy, holy, holy! The Infinite L-rd of Hosts! Blessed
be the Name of His glory!"

The choirmaster pulled Moses in front of their faces. Shocked.
Stunned. Chilled. Like a mountain of ice on a barbecue pit.

"Like I was saying," continued the choirmaster, "this is Moses. He's
a person, and he's here because, well…"

Stillness.

He got the words out fast and dry: "He's going to receive the Torah
in proxy for the Children of Israel."

At first, such silence as though all the sounds of a millennium had
been sucked in to the void. Then a popping here and there as the
more ethereal beings, unable to contain the revelation, dissolved
into flashes of cosmic dust. Then, the more robust, those who
survived, murmuring in protest, ranting louder and louder, and
then furiously in the most ultimate of all crescendos, like the roar of
a cosmic tsunami approaching the physiosphere, the howl of a
galactic hurricane whipped up in the Milky Way…

"Your precious, most hidden of all treasures!" they wailed. "A
treasure you have hidden for 974 generations before the world was
ever created, and 26 since then —and now You plan to fork it over
to EARTHLY BEINGS!!! CAST YOUR GLORY UPON THE
HEAVENS (Psalms, 8)! Let us—Your immaculate servants who
have sung Your praises all these ages, us who truly understand the
Depth of Your Wisdom and Holiness—let us have Your Holy
Torah! WHAT IS MAN THAT YOU SHOULD EVEN
CONSIDER HIM (ibid.)?!!"

The wails and howls soared in ever-rising amplitude until the entire
cosmic order resonated at supersonic frequencies, its energy level
treacherously approaching the point of auto-nihilation—when The

Boss, blessed be His Name and Glory ad infinitum, put His holy foot down (so to speak).

And so there was silence—sharp and sudden like the edge of a mighty cliff before the abyss.

The choirmaster, himself freshly re-incorporated into a more resilient spiritual form, wiped sweat from his brow and struggled to articulate the announcement he had just been instructed to make, "OK, everybody get to the benches. The concert is cancelled. We're going to have a legal debate."

Battling Angels

Scene changes are instant up there. It was not even a moment and the heavenly concert hall had become the heavenly court. A legal team was appointed to defend Moses and the Children of Israel, as well as an opposition to represent the angels themselves.

The defense began:

"It's not good enough to make all these claims of being better, demanding favoritism. If you wish that we angels should have the Torah for ourselves, you're going to have to play by the ground rules of Torah itself!"

The opposition smugly replied:

"And we shall: Baba Metzia, folio 108, second side. Cited by Maimonides, Laws of Neighbors 12…"

"Please get to the citation…"

"Very well: But first, observe exhibit A:"

A map delineating real estate properties was presented.

"You'll note that this landowner (A) has a portion of real estate for sale that borders on his neighbor's property (B)—over here. But he's nasty. Rather than deal with his neighbor, he sells it 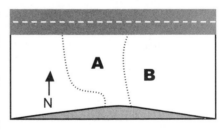 to some Joe off the street. So the neighbor is empowered by Torah law to go to this Joe, pay him his money, and nab the property for himself. Why? Because the Torah says, "You shall do that which is upright and decent" (Deut. 6:18). Upright and decent is to sell the property to your neighbor—because he's the one who can make the best use of it."

"And just what," demanded the defense, "has that got to do with our case?"

"Quite simple: The Torah is something heavenly and divine. We are too. That makes us neighbors. Earthly beings, aside from their many other serious defects, are very distant from spiritual matters. They have to struggle to grasp that which comes naturally to us. So we are neighbors and they are the distant Joe-off-the-street. Which gives us first rights."

The heavenly spectators couldn't help but let out a cheer of gladness. Their case seemed ethertight.

But then the defense retorted:

"You may consider yourselves erudite in the paths of Torah, dear opposition. But in this case, you have failed to note the gloss of the Maggid Mishna on that chapter in Maimonides. There, he cites the opinion of the "Itur" that these "rights of the neighbor" only apply to real estate. Torah, on the other hand, is not real estate, but moveable property."

The opposition: "And what, pray tell, is your evidence that Torah is moveable property?"

The defending angel rose to his full stature, as if exasperated: "Of course it's moveable property! If it weren't, you wouldn't have any complaint! It's being taken from *up here* in heaven and being given *down there* on earth!!"

In case anyone hadn't gotten the point by now, those words drove it home with a bite. One youthful angel had begun vibrating dangerously. Unable to contain his life-force in a passive mode any longer, he vaulted the bench and in flames of ionic crimson stormed above the frenzy:

"YES! THEY'LL HAVE THE TORAH DOWN THERE! EVERY TIME WE WANT TO PRAY, WE'LL HAVE TO WAIT FOR THEM TO GET OUT OF THEIR BEDS! WHEN WE WANT TO SANCTIFY THE NEW MOON, WE'LL HAVE TO GO TO THEIR EARTHLY COURTS TO FIND OUT WHAT THEY HAVE ESTABLISHED WITH THEIR PUNY BRAINS! WE WILL BE REDUCED TO NO MORE THAN GAGGED BACK SEAT DRIVERS, SHLEPPED AROUND BY THE WHIM OF THEIR PARALOGISTIC HUMAN MISHUGAS, COMPLETELY DEPENDENT FOR OUR VERY LIFE FORCE UPON THEIR CLUMSY, LACKADAISICAL FULFILLMENT OF MATERIAL MITZVAHS! WE, WHO STAND HERE EVERY DAY AND COMMUNE WITH THE DIVINE, FOR WHOM LIGHT AND REVELATION COMPOSE OUR VERY BEING, WE SHALL BECOME NO MORE THAN ACCESSORIES TO THOSE EGOMANIACAL, VULGAR, PHYSICAL BEINGS WHO WALK IN THICK DARKNESS, READY TO DENY THE VERY EXISTENCE OF THEIR OWN SOULS! NO! WE CANNOT LET THIS BE!!!"

Before the court clerks were able to haul the protestor away, he had already dissolved into the ether, returning to his source in the supernal void, yet another victim of cerebral overload for the day.

Beyond Panic

As the pandemonium subsided to the mallet of the chief justice, the opposition continued:

"We've had a chance to look over your sources, and, frankly, we're not convinced."

A sigh of relief rose from the crowd—in unison, of course.

"Certainly, the argument of the Itur would hold true in most cases, since the neighbor can always find similar goods elsewhere and bring them to his property. But in the case of the Torah, there simply is no replacement. Once it's gone, it's gone. There are no "similar goods". They will have it, and we shall be forced to descend to their realm to learn it from them. The entire flow of cosmic energy shall be in the hands of their good deeds and mitzvahs—and we shall only hope to assist them along. This, we assert, is unethical and contrary to Torah itself. Even the Itur has no reason to distinguish this from the law of real estate. The Law of the Neighbor's Rights still applies."

All heads nodded enthusiastically. The defense, however, was undeterred: "Even if your assertion can be supported, which we doubt, you will find yourselves helpless in countering our next defense. Our next argument is that these laws only apply to sales, whether barter or monetary. The Torah is not being sold. It's being given as an outright gift to the earthly beings. Look on the next side of the page there in Baba Metzia and you'll realize that none of these neighbor's rights apply to gifts!"

In the crowded aisles of the court, one angel whispered to another, "I told you we could never, never truly understand Him. Torah? An outright gift?!"

The opposition rebutted, indignantly:

"This is clearly a misrepresentation of the facts! The Torah is being sold, not donated!"

The Defense: "It's being given away! Gratis! In a nice box with ribbons and a birthday card!"

The Opposition: "It's being sold! For barter!"

The Defense: "I cite Brachot 5a, "Three good *gifts* did the Holy One Blessed Be He give Israel...Torah..."

The Opposition: "And I cite the same page in the same Gemora: The Holy One Blessed Be He says to Israel, "I have *sold* you my Torah..."!"

The debate shot back and forth as an electric storm across the heavens. Finally, it was conceded that some aspects of Torah were being given as a gift and others as a sale (and still other features as an inheritance). At any rate, the Law of the Neighbor still applied.

The defense was not yet stumped. Now Moses was being brought to the stand, not as the defendant, but as "Exhibit A".

The defense: "Behold the subject in question. Your first reaction was that this is an earthly being who has no business up here in our realm. But look again! You call this a man, I say he is truly an angel—and perhaps even greater!"

The defense was dangerously bordering on treachery, and knew it well. But that was a risk that had to be taken.

"This is the man who defied Pharaoh, who brought ten plagues upon the Egyptians, who spoke with G-d even while within the chambers of Pharaoh's palace! Split the Red Sea, made manna fall from heaven..."

"Big deal!" cackled the opposition, "Angels do similar things daily."

"…Led the Jews out of Egypt and through the wilderness for 50 days and put up with their kvetching!"

Now the angels were impressed. But the opposition protested, "So what does this have to do with our case?"

"Moses is no Joe off the street!" retorted the defense, "Just as we are neighbors to the Torah, *so is Moses!*"

The opposition was forced to yell over the ensuing commotion: "Deceit! Deflective tactics! You can't pull the wool over our eyes! He's not coming here to get the Torah for himself! He's planning to give it out freely to every Berel and Shmerel down there who wants to learn! And they are most certainly NOT OUR NEIGHBORS!"

"YES THEY ARE OUR NEIGHBORS!" The defense retorted. "They all—every one of them—have a spark of Moses within them! See Tanya, chapter 42. And furthermore, they are better than neighbors—they are RELATED to The Boss Himself! See Psalms, 148:14."

"This Law of Neighbor's Rights applies to relatives as well," snapped the opposition.

The Defense:	"Not according to the reading of the Baal Hilchot Gedolot, as brought by the Bet Yosef."
The Opposition:	"That's not the final ruling!"
The Defence:	"But did He not call them "my child, my first born" when He demanded that Pharaoh let them go? Rabbi Yitzchaak Alfasi claims that these laws certainly do not apply to children, and the Siftei Cohen contends that this is the halacha. They are all holy, divine beings themselves, their souls

carved out from under the Throne of Glory. They are capable of the most wondrous things! They deserve the Torah as much as we do!"

The Last Resort

The galleries were stunned. Their angelic sensibilities had been trashed. A backlash seemed imminent. Somebody in the opposition had to come up with something quick, or a riot would ensue.

"Hush! Children, be still!"

And so it was that an ancient being, one of those who had come into existence alongside time itself, rose to speak. All assumed a modality of quietness. His words, as follows, were perhaps the most revealing of the entire proceedings.

"If they are so holy," he softly spoke, "then I say, let them come up here. Let them ascend and share the Torah with us. After all, that is all we are asking: That the Torah should remain in the heavenly realms. It should remain a G-dly wisdom, a teaching of mystical abstractions that reveals the inner workings of the cosmos and allows us to bond with that essential force. They, too, may be permitted to transcend their corporeal bounds—through the efforts of meditation, fasting and prayer—and thereby rise to our spiritual plane and partake of this wonderful Torah with us."

The sagacious being stopped to ponder for a moment, as it beheld in a single vision all that would transpire over the coming millennia. And now he glowed with passion.

"But to allow this greatest of all treasures to descend to the material realm...to become manifest in the form of deeds bound by physical objects...performed by crude semi-animals formed from the earth who are filled with deceit and avarice...in a place where the Holy Torah could be mistaken for just another set of ethno-rituals or—yet worse—an exercise of cyber-acrobatics to feed the arrogance of silly men??!! For this the cosmos came into being? This should be the destiny of the Wisdom of the Most High??!!"

Choir Angels: "Holy, Holy…Blessed be…ad infinitum…"

The defense called for order, asserting it had one last argument. Perhaps a deflective tactic.

"Maimonides, ibid., chapter 12, halacha 5. Rosh on Baba Metzia 31. Brought as the final ruling in the Code of Jewish Law: The Right of the Neighbor does not apply in the event that the owner has a partner interested in purchase of the property."

The Opposition: "Now they are partners?"

The Defense: "They've already kept one Shabbat, and (Shabbat 109b): Anyone who recites the verses, "And the heavens and the earth and all their host were completed…" as the Shabbat enters becomes a partner with the Holy One Blessed Be He in the act of creation.

The opposition snapped back with a fury: "Now, I ask you: Is that fair? Of course they are partners! They have been given some preview mitzvahs already! Every mitzvah they do binds them in wonderful union with the Source of All Life—except that they remain **coarse physical beings**. But could you imagine—imagine it right now—if we, with our ethereal forms of light and divine energy, if we would be commanded to fulfill those same mitzvahs in our spiritual realm, as mystical meditations, as songs and holy communions? What greater unity could possibly exist? The Most Ultimate Oneness…"

The speaker for the opposition did not continue. In the excitement, he had already diffused his form and become absorbed into the Infinite Light. He wasn't the only one. The mention of such communion struck hard in the hearts of a multitude of beings, they too dissolving into the Nothingness. Other beings formed from the ambient energy and took their place.

Under these conditions, the debate could no longer continue, and so a vote was taken. An almost unanimous resolution was passed on to The Holy One Blessed Be He that the Torah be given to the angels, citing the law of Torah itself. Cheers of joy and gladness accompanied the clinking of glasses that echoed through the heavenly spheres.

The corks were still popping out of the champagne bottles, the band was warming up and the party was in full swing—when an unexpected response was announced. It came in the form of a cryptic memo—from The Boss:

"See Rashi ad loc., words beginning, "Akum, etc.".".

Angels are quick. "It means that the Torah has already been sold! Our case is no longer with The Boss, Blessed Be He, but with Moses, the buyer. He is hereby referring us to Moses to present his case!"

Moses, the man who defied Pharaoh, the man who argued with G–d and won, Moses took the stand. He cradled two massive carved stones in his arms. The heavens trembled.

Moses Takes a Stand

"This Torah about which we are arguing," he began, "what is written in it?"

"Yes, we've been through all that," mocked one of the angels. He elbowed a colleague, "Look who's trying to teach us Torah! Heh, heh!"

Moses continued, unperturbed, "I am the Lord your G–d Who took you out of the land of Egypt…"

His eyes scanned the hall. "So, you heavenly beings descended to Egypt?" With each word, his voice rose louder—but still controlled.

"You soiled your hands with bricks and mortar? Suffered the sting of the taskmaster's whip? Watched as your brothers and sisters and your very own children cried in pain and succumbed to the perverse cruelty of their oppressors?"

The Angels of Mercy poured out their tears. The Angels of Judgment shifted uncomfortably in their places. The Angels of Critical Analysis were frozen in stillness. The mockers were silenced.

Moses looked back down to read from his tablets.

"Let us see what else is written here: "You shall have no other gods before Me.""

He looked up. His voice was soft again. Soft like fine drops of acid upon a wound.

"Now, tell me, for whom is that written? For beings who perceive the Oneness of G–d as everyday reality? Do they require such stern warning, "Do not have other gods before Me"? Or is this meant for we who live in putrid, brain-confounding darkness, among nations who stray after literally hundreds of gods—each god with its seductive allure and missionary cult? Is it not we who are the ones to be told to have no other gods?"

His words echoed in the silent hall. Now Moses took his chance and made his words sharp as a dagger:

"I say, this Torah is not relevant to any of you in the first place!"

Indignation steamed over their heads in crackles and spurts. But no retort was heard.

Moses had his head back into those tablets. "Now let's see what's next...Taking G–d's name in vain! Now, why for heaven's sake would anyone want to take G–d's name in vain?"

The angels chewed on that one, but it didn't go down. Take G–d's name in vain? The words were meaningless to them.

"So let me explain: Earthly beings make business. I know you find that sort of thing rather loathsome, but that's what we do. In business, you sometimes have to take an oath, to assure the other party. Someone taking a false oath and using G–d's name..."

"Oh, no!" they screamed in horror. "Please don't go on!"

"Very well. You get the point."

He continued: "Now we get to the Holy Day of Shabbat. 'Six days a week you work...'"

"...And on the seventh," they rejoined, "a holy day of rest to the Eternal..."

"Rest?" countered Moses. "But when did you last work for six days?"

"We sing. Like Holy, holy..."

"I mean work! Like plow, sow, harvest, build and tear down—refashion the world about you through physical proaction!"

"You mean to say," enjoined one of the more thoughtful of the angels, "that you need the Torah more than we do. You need it for your very survival, considering the perilous conditions in which you live. Well, this is an interesting argument, and we are quite willing to argue this point…"

"No!" a flame-headed angel interrupted. "Torah is the life of all worlds—ours included! Without Torah, their world cannot go on, but neither can we! Imagine if all the effulgence of divine energy we received were put into their hands!? One letter of a mezuzah improperly written by one of these careless creatures, and entire universes could go under! One incorrect blessing could wreak irreparable havoc for giga-myriads of us! How could we allow our life force to be in their hands??!!"

"I don't think that's his point at all," opined another ethereal abstraction. "What he's been asserting all this time is that the precepts of the Torah are only applicable in the material realm. Now, this is preposterous: We all know that everything that exists in the material realm first exists in a spiritual sense here above, just as audible speech first exist as thoughts within the mind."

Angel heads were bobbing noddingly in accord.

"That angel over there, he is the life source of an oak tree on a hill on a small island. And that angel is the supernal origin of a squirrel that lives inside that tree. This fellow next to me is a rock at the bottom of the Aegean Sea. We are all the primal sources of all creatures below, from the inanimate to blades of grass to the wild and domesticated animals—even including the animal soul within Man. All the forces of nature and its elements, earth, water, air and fire, all are but mere reflections of our sublime intellects in their state of being here above. Every nuance of every wave of the sea, every bristle of leaves in the wind begins here…"

Chair: "Would you kindly cut the didactics and get to your point?!"

"…What I mean to say is that if they can fulfill these precepts in their lower realm, then all the more so can we in a spiritual sense. And we do: Every day we make our escape from an abstract Egypt—the bounds and limitations of being as we transcend to higher realms. Once a week, we keep the Shabbat by leaving the worlds created by divine speech and rising to the inner worlds of divine thought. We can do acts of kindness by bringing Divine energy lower. We can perform the sacrifices and prayer services by raising divine sparks higher. All through our meditation and song and great music…"

"Yes!" exclaimed an Angel of Excitement. "Whatever earthlings can do, angels can do better!"

Delight and gladness once again returned to the angels' court. Many cried together in unison: "Yes! He is right! Our mitzvahs will be so much more sublime than whatever they can do! Yes! The Torah belongs to us, the ministering angels!"

"And you, dear Moses," one turned sympathetically to the stand, "you need not feel left out: You or any of your people will be permitted to delve into the Paradise of Kabala, untie yourselves from your earthly bonds and join us in spiritual service!"

Heavenly harmony once again filled the cosmos. Pure, enchanting light flowed down from above. The dance choir had already risen and was carrying a protesting Moses on their shoulders, singing: "Holy, holy…blessed be…ad infinitum! Come sing with us!…"

It was then that the ancient being who had spoken earlier in our drama cleared his throat once again. It was ever so subtle, yet within the square root of a negative nanosecond the song and dance stopped. All heads turned respectfully. All aural senses were alert.

"I've been paying careful attention," he began, "and I don't think any of you have interpreted our dear Rabbi Moses correctly."

This was not what the angels had expected to hear. Energy levels sank sharply.

"He seems to have in mind something much deeper than you fathom. According to Moses," the venerable sage leaned on his luminous staff, "there is something special about the material realm that we have yet to realize. Something that somehow makes it the appropriate place for Torah to be—for our own good as well. I submit that we must allow him to continue."

Reluctantly, the heavenly court was forced to consent. Moses was plumped back down at his podium.

Moses Hits Where It Hurts

Moses was also hesitant about the next one. After all, it was certainly not Politically Correct. But the stakes were high. Moses looked back down into the tablets and read:

"Honor your mother and your father."

The angels saw what was coming. They began to wish they had never started all this in the first place.

"So??!!" his powerful voice shook the walls. "Where are your mothers and fathers?!"

"Umm, Moses…we don't do that sort of thing up here, we just…"

"So you admit!" Moses lurched forward, "You are creations of light! You have no mother or father! This miracle belongs only to us! Only in our world is found the Essence of the Infinite! Only in our world is reflected the most awesome, essential power of the Divine—the power to create being out of nothingness."

Even the most sublime of metaphysical intellects needed time to think about that—but Moses didn't give them a chance:

"And now see what else is written here: "Do not murder! Do not steal! Do not covet!…"—is there then jealousy up here? Do you fight one with the other? Do you struggle with an ominous darkness inside? Do any of you have these warped emotions that plague us below, this perverse drive to rebel against our very Source of Life and deny there is any authority outside of our own selves?!!"

"But, Moses, you take pride in this?!"

"Yes!" Moses retorted, "Because when we shall use the magnificent power of the Torah to resist, to redirect those ignominious energies to channels of holiness, to overcome darkness and transform it to light…we shall then uncover in the cosmos the Source of All Being Himself. For as He creates out of the void a being that feels absolute autonomy, we shall make that ultimate of being admit its nothingness. "

The angels were lost. Moses' eyes opened wide. "Look below," he uttered softly.

Secrets of the Depths Revealed

The lights were dimmed. Two hefty panels of the hall slid back revealing a panoramic screen. The aroma of heavenly buttered popcorn wafted through the ether. The angels munched away as the scene faded to a twilight-lit room where a young girl stood, stretching forth her hand to light a candle. The flame took hold and without warning, the heavens were filled with a blinding light.

"What is it? We have never experienced this light before!" they burst out.

"Keep watching," Moses told them.

On the screen was a table covered with wine, challah, and a mess of food. A family sat about, talking and eating. Inexplicably, the television was blank—even though the NBA finals were playing that night. The family began to sing—adults and children together. In their world, it seemed a cacophony of noise—but through the audio system up there resonated the sweetest of holy harmony.

"Who wrote that stuff?" the choirmaster demanded. "I've never heard anything like it!"

"Keep watching," said Moses.

They kept watching and they ahhed and ooed as earthlings sacrificed time from work to squeeze in a few prayers or catch a few words of Torah, as small children rejected candies because they weren't kosher, as these creatures transformed mundane activities of eating, sleeping and bodily functions into divine service with a simple blessing. With each scene, flashes of light jumped out from the material world and the objects of their deeds began to glow with divine emanation.

"What are those?" an astounded angel whispered,.

The ancient sage of the angels replied, his voice choking, filled with awe, "Those are the divine lost sparks. They fell from high beyond our world down and down to the earthly realm at the Dawn of Creation. These beings somehow have the ability to uncover them with their deeds, thereby transforming material objects into holy vessels."

"They make darkness into light!"

"Finite into infinite."

"Being into non-being!"

"You haven't seen nuthin' yet." Moses spoke, "Watch this!"

The date stamp at the bottom right of the screen indicated it was the eve of the final redemption. An earthly being sat and stared into a 17-inch LCD display, every once in a while clicking a button or typing on a keyboard. It seemed a dull activity, yet the angels could feel an essence-light emanating from those fingers and that machine, a light that seemed it could finally uncover the secret of Oneness within all the created realms.

"What is he doing?" begged the angels.

Moses explained: "The earthly beings created horrible tools of rampage and destruction, tools which they almost used to destroy all of their world. But now they have begun to transform these tools into good. This being is using an evolution of such a tool for connecting with other minds across the planet and learning Torah from them and with them, spreading kindness and wisdom. They call it "Internet"."

"You mean to say they use a tool created out of their most evil impulses to reveal the Oneness of their souls that transcends space and time?" they asked.

"You couldn't have put it better," replied Moses.

"You see," he continued, "you conceive of Torah as it would be in your realm: Now you have light—Torah, you imagine, would be just more of the same. More inner, more essential, but just light."

Now his audience was receptive. They realized that Moses had chosen an argument that satisfied their needs as well, and even beyond their highest expectations. They were to get "even more".

"But, for us," Moses went on, "Torah is more than light. When we take the Torah He gave us, we hold in our hands G–d Himself."

"Midrash Rabba, Leviticus 30,13," cited a scholarly angel.

"In the essence of the Torah is the Essence of G–d, and where is that revealed? Not here in the heavens, but there in the darkness, in the struggle to find good within the evil and godlessness."

The angels were about to begin their applause and sing a new song. But then...

"Wait!" shouted one of the Angels of Compulsive-Obsessiveness, "Have you all forgotten? What about the Rights of the Neighbor clause?"

"Baba Metzia, ibid. Maimonides ibid. 14.1," cited Moses. ""If the neighbor wants the property for planting seeds and the buyer bought it to build a home, the law does not apply." We are using the Torah to make the cosmos into a dwelling place for G–d in all His essence, a true home for Him. And that can only be accomplished by working in our realm, as demonstrated previously."

"And that," added the ancient of angels, a gleam in his eye, "is the purpose of all of Creation. Midrash Tanchuma, Nasso 16."

The applause burst forth as water breaking through a dam. The choir re-commenced its recital, glowing with crimson fire.

"Moses!"—one of the angels stepped forward to shake hands, "That was great! You know, your people will make great lawyers!"

Moses had not just won the Torah, he had won friends and allies. Our sages say that each of the divine beings gave him gifts and revealed their secrets to him. Even the Angel of Death, they tell us, whispered to him the secret of the holy incense—which he used later to prevent a plague.

And on that day, as the Eternal G–d descended on Mount Sinai, heaven came down to earth.

"The angels are jealous of he who struggles with darkness. They have light—but he touches the essence."

—*Bringing Heaven Down to Earth, Meditation 95.*

Sources: see Likutei Sichos, vol. 18, pg. 28.

THE ADAM FILES

Angels vs. Humans

The Kabala sketches the human being as an awesome confusion of the most lofty, sublime G–dliness with the most murky and darkest impulses. But this itself is the human's unique mission: To elevate and fuse every aspect of the cosmos, from the highest to the lowest, into a harmonious whole.

The angels, on the other hand—even the Angels of Truth—don't have the foggiest clue where to begin.

Part 1: The Shocking Truth About Heaven & Angels

In the wake of the startling revelation of the Sinai Files, a high-ranking official of the Department of Ministering Angels has daringly broken rank, revealing highly confidential information hitherto concealed to all but the most initiated. Today, on High Exposure, *as we approach the 5,758[th] birthday of Man, we present an exclusive interview with that senior official, Angel aob57648-3e vers. 6.2:*

Host: *Hello everybody and welcome to* High Exposure. *Tonight we have with us a senior official from the Department of Ministering Angels who has daringly broken rank to reveal highly confidential information to us, exclusively at* High Exposure. *And we're going to skip formalities and jump right into the mucky and murky realities right now.*

             Mr. Angel, you claim that the Sinai Files event was not the first attempt on the part of your colleagues to claim the central role in cosmic purpose at the expense of the human race. In fact, you say, this all really began much earlier than that.

Angel: At the very beginning.

Host: *So the original human being had barely a chance to get up on his feet, and there you were in that classic sibling-rivalry stance, viciously attempting to shake him to the ground. Wouldn't you expect that angels, with their massive intellects and lofty character, would be a step above that kind of thing...*

Angel: I understand your concerns 100%, Mr. Human, as do all my colleagues. You have to understand it was out of pure virtue and altruism that we filed our complaints. When we saw this pitiful mess that had been created, and...

Host: *Pitiful mess, eh? Hold on, Mr. Angel, let's back up a minute. We have confirmed information that you angels were consulted from the start about the creation of this first human being.*

Angel: Sure, that's true. It's no secret, either. Take a look in the Genesis account, you'll see where The Boss, May His Name Be Sanctified, says, "Let us make Man!" That "us" is a reference to none other than us angels.

Host: *So you willfully gave your endorsement to this project that you now call a "pitiful mess"? How do you explain that to our not-very-sympathetic audience?*

Angel: Endorsement? Like He needs our "Angelic Seal of Heavenly Approval"? He does whatever He wants!

Host: *So why did He deem it necessary to consult with you and your colleagues?*

Angel: That's just what we wanted to know. And we told Him right off, we said, "Listen, Almighty Boss, The cosmos and everything within it is all Yours. You do with it as You see fit." But He wouldn't take that for an answer. He said if He would just go ahead without consulting His employees, from whom would Alexander of Macedonia or Empress Katerina or Bill Gates or others who model themselves after Him have to learn?

Host: *So what did you advise?*

Angel: First we did our research. We requested a complete technical feature glossy on this Adam character.

Host: *He gave that to you?*

Angel: All He had to say was that this creature was going to have even more intelligence than we have. I can't hide the fact we were immediately skeptical. So we asked the Omniscient Creator, of Blessed Name, for a complete prognosis on this Adam-to-be and all his progeny for all generations. What exactly would they be doing with all this wisdom?

Host: *That must have been hard to sit through.*

Angel: And He laid it all out: Theft, avarice, homicide, warfare, genocide, sexual abuse, deforestation and environmental pollution, the public school system...

Host: *Please, you've said enough. The fact is, you gave approval and agreed to perform a job in which you actually had no confidence to begin with. Why?*

Angel: What were we supposed to do? Say, "Sorry Ultimate Boss and Master, we don't think it's a good idea"? Like I said: We had already told Him to go ahead and make His own decision. But no, He wanted us to debate the issue and present our findings.

Host: *In fact, we have a video recording of that debate—straight out of the ancient Midrash Rabba, chapter eight. And we're going to play the incriminating evidence right now:*

ChairAngel:	Okay guys. You get the ugly picture. Anyone have something good to say about this idea?
Debating Angels:	

ChairAngel:	Listen guys, this is a discussion. Someone *has to* say something good about the idea so we can discuss it.
Debating Angels:	
ChairAngel:	Listen guys, are we discussing or are we not discussing?
Angel of Kindness:	Okay, I'll say something.
ChairAngel:	Finally.
Angel of Kindness:	Ummm, ummm, ummm…
Angel of Truth:	He has nothing to say. Because there isn't anything to say.
Angel of Kindness:	That's not true! I can find something good to say about this human being creature! I know I can!
ChairAngel:	So go ahead, Kindness, that's all we're asking for.
Angel of Kindness:	Okay, once in a while, there's going to be a human being who will do something real nice, and…
Angel of Truth:	He won't really mean it.
Angel of Kindness:	He'll do it just for the sake of doing good.
Angel of Truth:	He'll do it for ulterior motives, like to look good or to show off or for some other utilitarian objective.

Angel of Kindness:	Sometimes, once in a while when no one is looking, one of them might do something real good, though. And what does it matter what the motives are—they're still good, beautiful deeds!
Angel of Truth:	What does it matter?! What does it matter?! Motives are everything! The Boss is creating a reality—and you are endorsing putting a creature into this reality who is full of lies and false motives!
Angel of Kindness:	But at least he'll be nice, sometimes.
ChairAngel:	Okay, we've got one vs. one. Any more opinions out there?
Angel of Justice:	Okay, I'll say something. I mean, this is a discussion, right? This creature will seek justice and do righteous acts, once in a while.
Angel of Peace:	And make wars about it.
Angel of Justice:	Sometimes you have to fight for a cause.
Angel of Peace:	They'll sure do that one good. They'll fight about everything. So here The Boss is creating a world and you're endorsing something that will do everything it can to tear that world apart!
ChairAngel:	Okay, score's two against two…

Angel: Please! Don't show me any more! I can't bear to watch what happened next!

Host: Perhaps you can just tell us.

Angel: You're right! It's all in that ancient Midrash! My buddies, the Angels of Truth, they were about to call witnesses and everything and trash the whole defense...

Host: *And then what?*

Angel: And then...they didn't get a chance! Before they knew what was up, The Boss had them cast down to the earth where their vote doesn't count! Can you imagine? He turned a blind eye to the facts so that He could create this being! A being created within the shadow of darkness and falseness!

So only the defense was left, who were shocked to find they had won a case they didn't really want to win. And then He went ahead and made Man before our disbelieving eyes.

Host: *Yet you yourself admit that this being has some redeeming qualities to it, don't you? After all, you actually witnessed the creation of Adam first hand, didn't you?*

Angel: Are you kidding? I was on the design team! We poured everything into this guy, everything that exists in the entire cosmos, upper and lower, plus the transcendent emanations, then all ten sefiros...

Host: *Ten what?*

Angel: Sefiros. Those are the modalities through which G–d creates worlds.

Host: *So what are they doing inside a human being?*

Angel: That's the whole point! This human being, it's got everything in it! It's a virtual microcosmos. In fact, that's really the core of this Adam thing: The ten sefiros.

Host: *How do they work?*

Angel: Ten sefiros are used for focusing unbounded light into well-defined, limited patterns. The particular form of the ten sefiros that Adam uses is called "Tikun". That's when each of the ten sefiros contains all the other ten. And they are all interconnected, as well. So the result is not only well-defined, but also produces an amazing harmony.

Host: *So you need these sefiros for creating worlds. So what does Adam do with them?*

Angel: Adam is the final focusing point for the Unbounded Light. He resolves everything into defined, discrete events and objects. We'll get to that later.

Host: *What about self-awareness? How does that happen?*

Angel Oh yeah—so we gave this thing three outer layers of thought, speech and action. That way, his inner mind could look at those outer layers and say, "Hey, that's *me* doing something!" That's where the self arises—humans think of those outer layers as being their true selves. Which is kind of ridiculous, but, look, it works really well.

Host: *Hold on. I thought Man was made in the image of G–d? Doesn't it say that somewhere? Why are you shaking your head at me with such a pitiful look?*

Angel: You must be a human. Don't you realize: HE DOESN'T HAVE AN IMAGE.

Host: *But doesn't it say...*

Angel: What it means is exactly as I've already told you. The image, i.e. design structure, that He used as the backbone for His entire creation—10 sefiros, etc.—He gave the soul of Man that image. I mean, it's a truly awesome piece of engineering.

Host: *Wait a minute. We're not so dumb. It says, "In HIS image, in the image of G–d"—not the image of creation...*

Angel: You don't appreciate the elegance of this design. Have you ever seen or heard or touched a masterpiece? When you get to the core of the thing you find the artist didn't just "do it". He invested his entire being into his work. Well, that's what you get with the ten sefiros. True G–dliness. That's why you can call Him Wise, All-Knowing, Kind, Mighty, Compassionate, etc....because He invested His Ultimate Oneness into those attributes in order to make a creation.

Host: *And that's what He put into Adam.*

Angel: He didn't put it. The Master Creator doesn't make things by "putting" them. He just mentions that they should exist and bingo, there they are. At least, as long as He so continues willing that they should exist...

Host: *So He mentioned this soul into Adam.*

Angel: No, no, no. That's how He did everything else. With Adam, He really blew it.

Host: *Oh, so that's where it went wrong.*

Angel: No, that was the best part. "He blew into his nostrils the Breath of Life." Get it?

Host: *Um, we humans are kind of slow.*

Angel: Here, take a deep breath. Now blow it all out at once, with all your strength. See how all your being is drained into that act? If it's deep enough, like when you suddenly sneeze, you actually go unconscious for a moment. It's not like just casually talking.

Host: *So that's another way of saying G–d invested His innermost into Adam.*

Angel: So to speak. That's what the Zohar says. I mean, you humans tend to take these things all too literally. As though we were talking about a Duncan Hines™ cake mix or something. That's why we don't generally go on public TV about them. But that's the basic idea.

Host: *So what went wrong?*

Angel: Everything.

Host: *But, I thought it was such a great design you guys had...*

Angel: Look, our job was software. How were we supposed to know that the hardware was to be made from mud? We pleaded with The Almighty Engineer of All Things to find a more fitting encasement for such an ultimate being. He assured us that this was the finest material possible.

Host: *It's not? Personally, I think the human body is pretty fabulous. I mean, all these years of research and doctors still haven't figured the thing out. It's totally amazing, the complexity and inner harmony, its beauty and...*

Angel: I know what you're going to say. It's public knowledge that the human body is actually a physical metaphor for the human soul, fitting it in every facet like a glove.

Host: *And we've got this wonderful diagram to demonstrate! [diagram]*

Angel: It's mud! You don't understand! You don't know what beauty is! You've never seen a spiritual body, like those of

96

us angels—when we're not appearing on TV. So you think this is beauty!

What you don't realize is this is but a faint, muddled reflection of the intricacies of the human soul warped into physical form. PHYSICAL! Get it! That's the whole issue here! It's not spiritual. There's no room for abstraction. It limits everything in quantifiable, concrete terms. The intelligence of the human soul could be grasping G–dliness, apprehending Infinite Light, absorbed in pure love and standing in absolute awe of the Essence of Being.

And instead it's stuck inside this gray meat patty processing data fed it by crude external perception devices that define everything in terms of measured, finite time and space!

Host: *You seem to be getting rather emotional about this issue. Angels are quite emotional, aren't they?*

Angel: Emotional! If you would see the tragedy, the outright debacle of it all, you would be trembling with despair! How could He have done such a thing? To throw such a fine piece of Himself, really—'cause that's what it is—into a coarse, physical, 100% finite encasement! Even the animals, their bodies and souls were manufactured together, in a single process. So they work so cleanly together. But for His most ultimate being He chose plain mud. It's so sad, such a tragedy. This soul could have been so much...

Host: *Here, take this tissue...*

Angel: From the highest, most lofty height to the lowest pit...

Host: *But if the software is so good, isn't that what counts?*

Angel: [blank stare] Perhaps you'd also like to run Windows NT on a 286? Or would you like to try ray tracing and 3D rendering on a Commodore 64?

Host: *Oh.*

Angel: It's worse. Much worse. It's bad.

Host: *So how did you get it to work?*

Angel: Well, we kludged[1]. We had to create an operating system that could interface[2] between them. We threw in a Vitalizing Soul to take care of running the basic body IO[3]

---

[1] **kludge** (also kludged as kluge)

/klooj/ [from the German `klug', clever; possibly related to Polish `klucz' (a key, a hint, a main point)] 1. n. A Rube Goldberg (or Heath Robinson) device, whether in hardware or software. 2. n. A clever programming trick intended to solve a particular nasty case in an expedient, if not clear, manner. Often used to repair bugs. Often involves ad-hockery and verges on being a crock. 3. n. Something that works for the wrong reason.4. vt. To insert a kluge into a program. "I've kluged this routine to get around that weird bug, but there's probably a better way." 5. [WPI] n. A feature that is implemented in a rude manner.

Adapted from the on-line hacker Jargon File, version 4.2.0. http://www.jargon.org/

[2] **Interface:** I use this word a lot, probably because I find it the most fascinating area of technology. Interface is when you have two things that operate in very different ways and you need them to communicate with one another. So you write some software or design something nifty that bridges the two. The computer has to interface with the printer—you write a printer driver. The human being has to interface with a computer—you give him a keyboard and a monitor and write software that makes the machine less user-abusive. G-d wants to communicate with human beings—He gives them a Torah. The G-dly soul needs to operate a human body—it gets an Animal Soul.

[3] Input-output. As in "whatever comes in must somehow come out."

stuff. Then we added an Animal Soul[4] to deal with data processing, and for an intelligence component and interface directly to the Breath-of-Life G–dly soul, we designed an intellectual soul—which actually has some elements of free choice and meta-consciousness. All as described in the "Book of Intermediates."[5]

Look, it's a kludge. It ended up so complex, with all this multitasking going on in all different directions at once, there are just so many bugs and things that can go wrong. Most of the time the Animal Soul just hogs all the processing time, and then the thing gets into such a mess...it's so, so limited...and He put a G–dly soul inside...can you imagine?

Host: *What kind of mess are we talking about?*

Angel: The main bug has to do with the Animal Soul creating this horrible filter that just gets thicker and thicker as it fills up with spurious data and noise, and that leaves no wavelength for the G–dly soul to stay bonded with its Source. But then the corporeal body itself provides such restriction and distortion as well. Fortunately, the essence can't be destroyed, but the rest of it, boy oh boy...well, look at yourself for example...

So that's when we posted an official notice of litigation. We cited The Almighty Blessed Be He's original

---

[4] **Animal Soul:** This makes up the fundamental personality of the human being—its perception, emotions and standard reactions to its environment. The Tanya (see next note) discusses the struggle that develops between the G-dly Soul and the Animal Soul.

[5] A.k.a. Tanya, volume 1. Classic work of Rabbi Schneur Zalman of Liadi (1745–1813) that begins by describing the layers and functions of the human psyche in detail.

statement that this being was to contain even more wisdom than us. Since we had been employed for the design process, we felt that statement was a contractual obligation and what had now ensued was without legal justification.

So, see? Really it was our compassion for Man's pathetic state that drove us to demand a justification for the act of his creation. That's when The Almighty suggested a contest—between us and Adam.

Host: *Now, let's get to this contest. Describe the scene for our audience.*

Angel: It was awesome. And it was exciting. We all crowded into this theatre that had a device to project 3D views of physical beings into the spiritual realm for all to perceive. The most sublime intellects amongst us, I mean like the Angel Gabriel and the Angel Michael and all the Supernal Chariot fellows, they took the front rows. The rest of us stood in the back munching the popcorn in total awe. I mean there's just nothing we World of Formation guys—or even World of Primal Creation guys—can add to the super-intellects of those World of Emanation pros.[6] There's just no comparison. But we wanted to watch.

Host: *And what did you see?*

Angel: Physical beings. And we had to give them names.

Host: *Like a matching game.*

Angel: That's right. The kind you give little kids in kindergarten, where you show them a page of animals and animal names

---

[6] See page 278.

and ask them to match the names with the animals. That's what it was.

Host: *And for this you needed the Angel Michael?*

Angel: Don't get sassy, now. You've got to remember, this was the first time in cosmic history anything had been named. Those cutesy animals down there in the physical Garden of Eden, all of them were fresh off the production lines.

Host: *Sounds more like Madison Avenue than a matching game. You just look at the target audience, find a catchy name...*

Angel: NO! NO! NO! What do you think we are—Mattel Toys or something?! We had to MATCH them with names. The names already exist, just that they had never been called these names. That's what we had to do.

Host: *But how could names exist if nobody had ever called them?*

Angel: Such a shame. You know, your great-grandfather, Adam, he knew all this stuff. I guess it just didn't filter down to you—what can you expect with all that OS noise, physical device distortion and all? Anyways, we have a beautiful 3D multimedia show ready to run that will make the whole thing clear.

Host: *Ok, let's run that now...*

Angel: Sure, just put these goggles over your eyes. Now bring the phones down snuggly over your ears. Here, let me place this device over your heart..

Host: *Heart?*

Angel: Yes. This show has been known to be quite breathtaking in the past. We need to monitor your vital signs...

Host: *Is that also the purpose of those electrodes poking out of the helmet into my brain?*

Angel: Well, some of them. Most are mind-altering devices...

Host: *Mind what!!? Hey, I thought this was just an animated 3D model...*

Angel: The only true model is the real thing itself. This device allows you a lucid view of reality.

Host: *If I'm supposed to see reality, then what are you doing altering my mind?*

Angel: At present, your consciousness is highly limited. It utilizes a filter that blocks out the objective reality for a more palatable, subjective one. Not really your fault—its just that you are so encumbered by space/time parameters, you only see that which relates to space and time in their most quantifiable state. Couple that with your egocentric interpretive functions and your reality is way out of whack.

        Now, for a moment, you're going to see raw, lucid reality as the prophets see it at the time of prophecy, or other great tzaddikim at their most sublime moments. Something approaching what the Children of Israel experienced when, at the ultimate multimedia show at Mount Sinai, they "saw the sounds and heard the sights."

Host: *Will I become a prophet this way? Do I get to see next year's stock market reports?*

Angel: Due to the minimal amount of briefing and preparation you've had, we'll be glad if you survive a few nanos and remain capable of producing intelligible speech. Think of it as similar to running all the turbo-electric power of Niagara Falls through a penlight.

If you do retain your faculty of speech, however, you'll describe to our audience the entire experience. You will retain intellectual property rights over your description and be entitled to publish in major newspapers and journals internationally, as well as appear on Oprah.

Are you willing?

Host: *Sounds good.*

Angel: Then sign here.

Host: *I'll be glad to sign, right after a word from our sponsor, and then we'll be returning with part two of..... The Adam Files!*

Part 11: Secrets of the Cosmos Made Easy

Host: *Here we are back at the Cyberspace Show, discussing the Adam Files in an exclusive interview with that senior official, Angel aob57648-3e version 6.2 .*

When we left, I was about to don a mind-altering device in order to view the backstage "reality behind our reality." Due to concerns of the TV hosts' union insurance underwriters and the failure of our lawyers to find an agreement to satisfy all parties, that plan has been dropped. Instead, Mr. Angel here has agreed to provide us with a reasonable simulation, utilizing some amazing technology leaked from Heaven Technologies Inc., exclusively for our show.

Mr. Angel, explain to our audience just what is this device.

Angel: Here we have a miniature creation device. Also known as an *Isifier™*. It utilizes 10 coordinated light sources that project a total of twenty-two varieties of energy types that combine in about 22-to-the-23rd-power combinations to form all types of objects that comprise an entire world and all its history.

Host: *OK, so let's try it.*

Angel: So I just switch on the power and...

Host: *Hey that's neat! Sort of a 3D-hologram effect! There are little animals and people walking around in a very realistic environment. I can even see the vegetation growing as we talk! Boy, where do you store the mega-data for all those images?*

Angel: They're not just images. They are kinetic-tactile objects.

Host: *You got to be kidding! Well, then, let me just lean over and I'll tap this little guy on the head...*

Little Guy: Hey, you up there! Pick on someone your own size!

Host: *Wow! They're interactive, too!*

Angel: Don't get abusive, now. They have feelings and intelligence and even consciousness as well. Just ask one of them and you'll see.

Host: *Hey, you! Do you have consciousness?*

LGuy: I'm not sure. Let me ask Joe here. Joe, do we have consciousness?

Joe: Consciousness? You still believe in that stuff? I told you before: If you can't see it, touch it or hear it, it doesn't exist. All that's up there is gray matter and physiological behavior-response! No consciousness.

LGuy: Joe says we don't have consciousness of our existence. Just gray matter.

Joe: Hey! Who are you talking to?

LGuy: Oh, there's some giant being up there in outer space that...

Joe: How many times have I told you? There are no giant beings in outer space!

LGuy: Hey, Mr. Giant? Sorry, but I'm going to have to stop talking to you. Joe says you don't exist either. And he's a scientist, so he should know.

Host: *Mr. Angel, this is impossible! How can a couple of light sources project tactile, interactive objects that have all the qualities of us human beings?*

Angel: Oh, this is only a miniature simulation. The one that makes you and your world is actually larger than this.

          Also, this one simply runs within the pre-existing time and space parameters of your world. The real thing inits those parameters ex-nihilo as well. If you like, I could show you one that uses alternative parameters to time and space…

Host: *Awesome! But first, let's get into the technology behind this wonderful device. In very simple terms, how does it work?*

Angel: Sure, well it's basic Kabala stuff, like you read about in the Book of Formation. Like I said, there are 22 forms of energy that start out in 10 express statements. They then branch out through various algorithms to make up virtually unlimited configurations of those 22. Each configuration becomes an isifying[7] force for a particular event or object.

For example, see those miniature waves coming into the miniature seashore in our miniature world here? The ocean has a configuration of forces that creates it, waves have another one, and each formation of a wave at each point on its journey to the shore has a distinct configuration of some set of the 22 forces to create it.

Host: *Twenty-two—now that's an interesting number. Does that have any relation to the 22 letters of the Hebrew alphabet?*

Angel: Now you're getting on the ball. In fact, they are the original 22 letters. The Hebrew letters you use in reading, writing and in speech are the most direct physical manifestations of these 22 energy forces. Their spoken sound and their written form are reflections of the particular characteristics of each letter.

---

[7] Like *vivify*, but with *is* instead of *viv*. Okay, I made the word up. Look, in Hebrew you can conjugate the verb "to be" this way. So why shouldn't I do it in English?

Host: *Awesome! So the energy-combinations of those 22 basic building blocks are like words!*

Angel: Precisely. And 22 letters make a lot of words. But then, those words have babies…

Host: *Babies?*

Angel: Sure. They transform by switching their letters with other letters with similar sounds, or according to the place of the letters in the Hebrew alphabet, or according to the numerical value of the letters. Each transformation decreases the energy intensity level of that word.

Host: *And do those babies have babies?*

Angel: It goes on and on. The energy has to be really stepped down. I mean, you can't have some blade of grass, or a worm, or some human brain created with the same energy level as say a galaxy or an angel like me. So the energy has to go through many generations to reduce those levels.

Host: *So how many creations in total can you get out of 22 letters?*

Angel: Well, you can have a lot of duplicates this way—as long as the parents are different. There's really no limit. But, in this universe we're talking in right now, let's just say it's enough for every subatomic particle there will ever be in this universe.

Host: *I'm impressed. But still confused. I mean, I can get describing a whole world using a sophisticated 22-base branching scheme like you just described. But you've got a little world here that I can see, touch and feel. How do these energy-combination word-thingies create tangible objects?*

Angel: That's precisely the difference between using numbers and using words. Numbers are just quantities. If I give you all the numbers that describe the chemical make up of your favorite ingestible substance...

Host: *Rocky Road ChocoMaple Ice Cream with real pistachios.*

Angel: ...no matter how well you digest those numbers, it won't give you the sensation of eating ice cream. But if I describe it in words...

Host: *...the initial numbing, creamy cold impact on the tongue and palate, followed by a burst of sweetness from the taste buds, then the finer sensitivity of the olfactory glands kick in—first detecting the bitter-sweet chocolate, then detecting the hint of maple—and finally, the crunch of those pistachios exploding into new bursts of colorful flavor, all of it flowing down the esophagus to develop a sickening, heavy feeling in the digestive tract...*

Angel: You see, words carry qualities, as well. So words can create.

Host: *But an entire world?*

Angel: It's sort of like how your own words work. After all, you are made in the Divine Image, remember?

Host: *Glad you remembered that.*

Angel: So, let's say you had—just for the sake of our little explanation here—that you had a really deep feel for all this Kabala stuff we're talking about, that you really understood it all. So then, let's say you wanted to communicate not just the ideas, but that deep, inner feel for it all—that you had a need to express all this to others, say that they would catch just the same sort of inspiration as you.

So you would come up with words to express those ideas. But words wouldn't be enough. You would need metaphor. You would need story. You would need varied voices to explain the ideas. You might make up a whole crazy story, maybe even a talk show with some goofy host and a weird angel, just to get this inner understanding out there.

Host: *And then those characters in the talk show might even think they were for real?*

Angel: Well, that's going a little far. But you get the idea. Your words take a numinous feeling for an idea and transform it into an entire world that you and others can relate to and appreciate.

Like I said, that's because your words are a reflection of how the Divine words work, except those work with infinitely more creativity. But the mechanism is the same.

Host: *Ingenious! Listen, Mr. Angel, we have to talk after the show. I've got a brother-in-law who works with venture capital, and you know they're always looking for hi-tech stuff. Especially if you could make it have something to do with the Internet and throw in a couple more buzz words...*

Angel: Oh, you wouldn't be able to manufacture this on earth...

Host: *Well, you angels could do it. Listen, we're talking major, major stuff here. I can see the ads now: "Create your own worlds!" "Play G–d in the comfort of your own living room!"*

Angel: We couldn't do it either. Both you and I are missing the most basic element of existence...

Host: *But, I told you, I can get all the venture capital you need...*

Angel: There is a higher force than venture capital. There's Him.

Host: *Don't worry about him. There are antitrust laws. We'll copyright the look and feel so reverse engineering won't help. Besides, we'll sell him non-voting shares and let him talk to all our stockholders over a big screen.*

Angel: Not him. I mean **Him.**

Host: *Him?*

Angel: **HIM.**

Host: *Oh, that Him. Can't do it without Him?*

Angel: That's the whole secret behind the creation something-from-nothing bit. You see, everything else is a something that has another something from where it comes. Whatever those somethings could create would still not be something from nothing. But He Himself has no source, so He is not a something, really, at all. He just is. Therefore, He is the only one that can create a tangible something just out of nowhere. See Tanya, book 4, chapter 20.

Host: *Why can't He just let some of us have this power to create ex-nihilo for a moment? I mean, imagine the thrills, the empowerment, the volume sales...*

Angel: That's ridiculous. If He gave you the power to create, it wouldn't be creating out of nothing, would it? You would be creating it out of that power He put inside you.

But with **Him**, it's not that way. There's no power to create, no potential world. Nothing. Just an ultimately simple Thereness. And that's the power behind those Divine, creative words—He is there within them.

Host: *Then where do you guys fit into this whole system?*

Angel: Glad you asked that, because that's crucial to understand for a proper understanding of the Adam vs. Angels conflict.

We don't generate this system. We're just part of it. We get created by combinations of the 22 letter-forces just as you do. Then we have some management positions within it. Even then, we don't really have any authority because He insists on micro-managing absolutely everything.

Host: *So what makes you a refined spiritual being and me a coarse, physical object?*

Angel: It's a quality issue. You see, there are words and there are words. There are the words you speak to other people, and there are the far richer, luminous words that you hear inside your own mind. The words that create us are more of the latter sort.

As a matter of fact, let's demo that right now. Let's turn back to this little world we've generated. Now this dial here adjusts the quality of the signal. I'll turn it up ever so slightly so as to reduce noise and increase fidelity...

Now, ask your question again.

Host: *Hey, little guy, do you have consciousness?*

LGuy: There is only the Higher Consciousness of Supernal Being. What you see is a mere reflection of that awesome light. And let us praise the Source [breaks into ethereal singing]. Halleluja!

Angel: Or we could turn it down ever so slightly, like this, thereby coarsening the quality of the vitality that enters the system. This will also conceal the origin of the beings from them, to the point that they will not recognize that anything at all exists outside of their own little realm.

Host: *Sounds like that's where that Joe guy was at already.*

Angel: Joe was an angel compared to where those two are at now. Go ahead. Try getting into a conversation with them.

Host: *Um, Little Guy...*

LGuy: Whadja want?

Host: *Excuse me, but...*

LGuy: Cut the excuses and get to the point.

Host: *Do you have consciousness?*

LGuy: Depends. How bad you need it and how much you willing to pay for it?

Host: *Actually, consciousness is an awareness of being...*

LGuy: Just tell me who the market is and what sort of volume sales you expect to make.

Host: *Angel! He's making fun of me!*

Angel: I better turn that function back up before this guy gets you beeped off the air.

Host: *So, back to our subject, you're telling me that you and I and all of us and all this about us is nothing more than G–d thinking and speaking, thereby creating this Divine flow of energy that makes us happen. And that's what it means, "He spoke and it was!"*

Angel: So to speak.

Host: *And once He's spoken His words, well, here we are.*

Angel: In a limited way.

Host: *Limited?*

Angel: Yes, because the words must be constantly flowing from Him, just like an electric current. For example, let's say I would turn this device here all the way to zero flow...

LGuy: No! Don't do that! Joe, they're threatening to unplug our world! We'll cease to exist in a flash!

Joe: There you go with your doomsday stuff again.

Angel: ...or I could just retro-trash Joe. Like this...

Host: *Hey, little guy! Where did Joe go?*

LGuy: Joe? Who's Joe?

Host: *How come he doesn't remember Joe?*

Angel: The energy-combination that creates Joe is beyond the time-space parameters of the little guy's world. So when it is removed, Joe's past is gone as well. In that world, Joe now never existed.

Host: *Couldn't you just play around a little with Joe's particular configuration so he gets a little more sense in his head?*

Angel: Sure. That's what you call making a miracle. You just temporarily change around a few forces and allow things to work differently for a while. You'll find allusions to the mechanics of it even in the Talmud. But the Boss likes to avoid that whenever possible, saving it for only special occasions. He likes the natural order better, since it's much more elegant.

Of course, tzaddikim play that game frequently. That's how they heal the sick, make golems, cause vinegar to burn like oil—all that stuff.

Host: *So you can remove stuff, you can modify it—how about adding on? Can you introduce new elements into this environment without upsetting the system?*

Angel: Well, let's just enter a few new data structures here through the keyboard...We'll introduce a few grand firs and a maple tree, one of them a stump to achieve realism, and over in the distance there we'll add a mountain range and a lake...

Host: *Hold it! This is heavier than damming the Yangtse! What about the environmental impact study? Do you know what kind of fluff this is going to get you from the Green Lobby?*

Angel: Everything's under control. We've got unlimited teams of ecology balancing angels built into the system to manage all the necessary adjustments. As a matter of fact, nobody within the system will notice a thing out of place!

Host: *That's ridiculous.*

Angel: Go ahead and ask. I even put Joe back so you can get a scientific perspective.

Host: *Hey, Joe!*

Joe: [shaking his head, mumbling to himself] Maybe I've just been thinking too hard. It's those voices again.

Host: *I mean, hey little guy! Where did those mountains come from?*

LGuy: Mountains? Mountains don't come from anywhere! They're just there!

Host: *Well, they had to get there somehow!*

LGuy: Hmm, I guess you're right. I'll ask Joe the scientist. Joe, how did those mountains get there.

Joe: Those? Oh, that's the Galapuskian Range. They were formed in the volcanic upheaval of the Epidermical Era which ended 150 million years ago.

Host: *Listen, guy, tell Joe he's off his rocker! Those mountains weren't even there yesterday! They appeared just now, along with those trees you're standing next to.*

LGuy: Huh what?

Host: *Sure. Surprise, surprise! Didn't notice those trees you're standing next to? So when did those get there, eh?*

LGuy: Well, I can remember climbing that big maple as a youngster. And the other whatever-you-call-them big trees, well, they look pretty old to me. Joe, any idea how old these trees are?

Joe: Simple! We just count the rings on this stump, which appears to be of the same age... looks like about 140 years old. Apparently, however, not virgin growth.

Host: *It's not true! That stump was just created this very moment! And so were all those other ones, and even the mountain range over there! You guys are making this all up!*

LGuy: You know, Joe. I've decided you were right all along about those voices and talking to super-beings out in the sky.

Host: *I've lost credibility, just by saying the truth.*

Angel: Join the crowd.

Host: *But, what's with their memories? Did you adjust those too?*

Angel: Their memories are perfectly intact. That small being did climb that maple as a child. When we created the maple, we created its entire past, and that event was included in it.

Host: *And that's why that stump had all those rings! And the mountain range...*

Angel: Well, that's not within their living memory range or recorded history. But if their world had actually developed on its own within the same parameters and conditions as it has now, their estimate wouldn't be so far off.

Look, that's not the point. The point is that now you can see how everything within this little world before you is nothing more than manifestations of the energy configurations input into it through this device. Even its past, its sense of time and space and consciousness. And that should give you an inkling of how your world here is sustained in a similar fashion.

Host: *Wow! So that's the real reality! But don't we see all this! Why can't we see these words of energy configurations that are constantly creating us at every moment?*

Angel: Oh, well that's a user-interface issue. The Blessed Creator in His Infinite wisdom wanted to hide all the engineering from the end users. A transparent interface just wouldn't have allowed any room for free choice. You wouldn't feel like you were in a real world.

Host: *Ok, so you had to place something between the user and the raw code—but couldn't He have made it a little more user friendly?*

Angel: Look, I admit it's not exactly intuitive as shipped. You need a manual to figure out what to do and what not to, and even that wasn't delivered for the first 2448 years of existence. But it could have been worse. I mean, he could have hired some hick company in Redmond, WA to design the user interface.

Host: *No! Not that!*

Angel: And things eventually work out. It just takes some fine tuning. Listen, very soon there's going to be a whole new reworking of the user interface. Things are going to be 100% intuitive. The whole system will become transparent. Downright luminous.

Host: *Any inside rumors on the shipping date?*

Angel: It shipped already. With the manual you got over 3300 years ago. You've just been installing it ever since.

Host: *You mean all those 613+ instructions are for fine tuning the Creation?*

Angel: On the ball again. You must have been reading those Sinai Files.

Host: Talking about the Sinai fiasco, we're going to be getting into an even earlier fiasco, this time centering around a contest between the ministering angels and the Primal Man. The stakes were as high as they can be and the competition even higher. Mr. Angel here has brought an under-the-table video that reveals all. We'll be showing that to our audience with a running commentary from the experts, just as soon as we get back from our sponsor.

Part III: Showdown at High Noon

Welcome back to the Cyberspace Show.

Last we left off, Angel aob57648-3e version 6.2 was prepared to unveil a clandestine video of the notorious Angels vs. Adam contest, revealing the attempted ploy of the Ministering Angels to depose Mankind from his central position in creation. Let's roll that video now:

The upholstery in the theatre was in good shape, as would be expected considering that the world of the angels had only been created in the last few days. But it was crowded, and it was intense.

Standing arrangements (angels don't sit) were by ethereal plane, this being a cross-boundary, inter-reality theatre. In the highest realm of existence stood the Supreme Angels of Kindness, Judgment and Compassion (aka Michael, Gabriel and Raphael). Oblivious to the successively lower realms beneath them, they stared intently into the projection capsule, focusing all their massive, perfect intellect onto the case at hand.

The case at hand was a four legged physical being, projected into their sublime ethereal world for observation purposes. Their task was to call this being a name, and for the life of them they could not...

Angel Michael: Angel Gabriel, run by me the data you've got on this being, again. Maybe if we co-analyze...

Angel Gabriel: Basic element is mud. That's a composite of all four basic elements of fire, air, water and earth as they exist in the lowly physical realm, with a preponderance of the latter two.

Angel Raphael: Amazing! In direct contradistinction to us, who are entirely fire and air...

Gabriel: ...and of course, fire and air in their totally non-physical, abstract form.

Michael: Now that takes care of its substance—what about its form? We've got to have some analysis on that.

Gabriel: It is entirely quantifiable within the measurements of three dimensional space, within which it excludes the possibility of any other physical form. It also leads a single point existence on a linear path of time.

Raphael: You mean, it only exists at one single point in time at any given moment?

Gabriel: And in only one perfectly defined space—with absolute exclusivity on that space as well. Physical objects are not able to share the same space.

Raphael: Wow! I never imagined the Light could descend that low, into such severe limitation.

Gabriel: This is the ultimate limitation.

Raphael: So then, how could they exist if there is no room for harmony or shared data? Existence is a product of life-flow, and that could only be in something that is capable of surrendering some of its self-ness.

Michael: I think you've hit on something, Raphael. That is definite evidence that there is life within this being. But where, and—more crucial to our task—what??

Gabriel: Now that you mention it, I can perceive a life force arising from this being...

Michael: And I can detect the flow descending into it. I believe it is emanating, initially at least, from the animal to the left on the Divine Chariot.

Gabriel: Right.

Michael: Left.

Gabriel: Right, left.

Raphael: Then that angel should be able to name this creature!

Michael: I have a better way. Gabriel, look up the combination of divine powers creating the angel to the extreme left of the Divine Chariot.

Gabriel: Left, right?

Michael: Right. Left.

Raphael: Right or left?

Gabriel: Left.

Michael: Right.

Gabriel: Left. That reads, "Shin, Vav, Resh." "ShOR."

Host: *That's it! They've done it! "Shor!" —That's Hebrew for "Ox"! Holy Cow! They've found the source of the animal up above and figured out its name that way!*

Angel: Hold on—it's not so simple. Figuring out is one thing. Calling it a name is another.

Host: *Huh?*

Angel: Wait and see what happens next.

Raphael: The ShOR Angel is all lit up now! Looks like a hyper-conductive conduit of energy has been led through it!

Michael: That's just the effect of Gabriel calling its name. He's brought it into transparent interface with its source. It's bonded now—at least temporarily. So its source is shining through at full power.

Gabriel: Now if we could only achieve that with this mud-being here. That's the challenge.

Raphael: Sorry. Don't see any luminance happening there. Just a dumb four-legged chunk of meat staring at us while chewing pre-chewed grass.

Host: *I don't get it. They've got the name and it works. What's the problem? Give them their little gold figurine and let them go home!*

Angel: Of course you don't get it. They've got something you don't have.

Host: *Fluffy wings and flashy halos?*

Angel: Intellectual integrity. They can't call it a name until they can actually see that element of spirituality within it on its own level. Right now, their calling it a name doesn't accomplish anything. They've got to call the name into it because they really see it there. That way they will actually connect it to its source.

Michael: We're not going to be able to achieve anything with that thing from here. We're too elevated. We need to contact one of the lower realm angels with the data and have him do it.

Raphael: Oh, no! We can't do that! I tried it just yesterday. I appeared to this lower-realm being who receives his energy through me. He looked up and thought, "Wow. This must be some sort of weird mirror. That looks like an exaggerated reflection of me, in qualitatively expanded terms." I had to tell him the truth, that no, just the opposite, he's just a reflection of me, lacking dimensions 25 and 26 and qualitatively totally superfluous at relatively zero energy.

Gabriel: What happened to him when you did that?

Michael: I don't think I want to hear.

Raphael: He was just gone. He shifted into ecstasy mode and the energy levels were just too high and...look, I didn't know...the world's just been created after all...how could I have known the poor little guy was without overload protection?

Michael: Here, have this tissue...

Gabriel: What a way to go.

Michael: OK, so angels are not upwardly mobile without serious overload consequences. But can they move downward?

Gabriel: Just who are you planning to send down there?

Michael: Well, this ShOR fellow you've just so graciously connected, what I'm thinking is if we send him down...

Gabriel: ...since he knows his own name...

Michael: ...he should be able to draw it into himself. You might call it "auto-connectivity."

Gabriel: Of course, we could always give him some prompts. Sounds interesting.

Raphael: But what will happen to him once he's down there? Look, if we don't get him back up...

Michael: We better look at the compensation clause in his contract. Gabriel, anything about terminal materialization in there?

Gabriel: It's not necessary. I've figured out a way we can send him down to the most absolutely physical realm and yo-yo him back up immediately once his mission is accomplished.

Raphael: Amazing!

Gabriel: Apparently, the Boss, Blessed Be He, left a door open for that sort of thing, meant for future cases such as visiting Abraham, rescuing Abraham's nephew, helping Ethel Goldberg's husband keep his job despite himself, and similar such cases.

Raphael: And just who is He planning to use on those missions?

Gabriel: You don't want to know.

Raphael: First of all, it does make a difference. Secondly, if it's His sublime mission, then the descending beings will obviously remain intimately bonded throughout their journey. But who says we can ensure that on our little escapade?

Michael: My dear colleagues, we all understand the risks involved in this experiment. But on the other hand, we also are well aware of the implications if we fail.

Raphael: Michael, winning isn't everything.

Michael: Winning is the least of my concerns, Raphael. The earthly beings must be connected to their source, or else the whole of creation will remain a futile exercise, terminated before it even has a chance to achieve maturation. Our continued existence depends on a smooth and constant circuitry of energy connecting the highest with the lowest and then moving back up reciprocally.

Gabriel: The current I am aware of is DC—a direct, unilateral current from Above to Below. I perceive it as pulsating in an on/off modulation. We become aware of the supernal void from which we extend, then, as we surrender our state of being to that all-transcendent reality, we are renewed with the Divine Will that we exist. Which brings us once again back to the awareness of the Higher State, and so on at every nanosecond.

Raphael: Gabriel, put a hold on the meditations! You just burned up 10,000 hosts of lower realm angels! I was only able to re-corporealize them through an extended turbo-compassion flow.

Gabriel: Sorry, Raphael, but that's all just part of the dynamic. You're going to have to get used to working this way, 'cause that's what we're stuck with for the next 6,000 years.

Michael: Gabriel, you are certainly correct that the primary current is DC. Nevertheless, there is a secondary, yet more important current—namely the Reciprocal Light. It reflects the very purpose of creation as well as the Absolute Oneness of the Supreme Being, as it implies that there is nothing outside of His Oneness, even to the very lowest of worlds.

Gabriel: The DC stuff isn't enough?

Michael: The flow that comes directly from Above is rationed and highly limited. What comes from below brings new, extra and transcendent light into our hollow. Also, the DC energy can only endure temporarily without some sort of flow being initiated from below.

Raphael: So what creates the AC current?

Gabriel: I believe we'll have a demo of that right now. Gabriel, zoom that camera on the Adam being, right away.

[Adam is looking about the parched, barren landscape, shaking and scratching his head. He then looks up, pondering deeply. Finally he gestures down to the ground while still looking up, and yells, "Needs watering!"

[Up in the heavens, all is shaken and angels light up in neon colors as a tremendous surge of energy rockets through them on its upward path, and then again, even more, as the energy pours back down in torrents.

[Below, a thunderstorm ensues and vegetation sprouts up from the ground. Adam smiles and celebrates, waving kisses to Above.]

Raphael: [still recovering] Michael, that was wild!

Gabriel: Michael, you still with us?

Michael: I'm just experiencing this total sense of relief...

Raphael: We never had anything like that energy before. It was an entirely new sensation. How can we get more? Where does it come from.

Michael: It originates from the base, material world. There is infinite light hidden there, far beyond anything that can descend directly from Above.

Gabriel: Hold it! If they have an infinite light, then why are they so base and material?

Michael: I know it sounds counter-intuitive, but you'll just have to trust me on that one. In order to generate tactile-kinetic physical material out of our spiritual reality, the Infinite Light had to be engaged in full force. It's there, but in ultimate concealment.

Gabriel: Sounds like another of those "highest things are revealed in the lowest" paradigms.

Michael: You got it. Only the most ultimately infinite could create the most ultimately finite. Generating more and more spiritual worlds—well, any old divine light can do tetra-realms of those. But to create a tangible clump of dirt out of spiritual energy, you need the Absolutely Infinite to pull that one off.

Raphael: I don't see any infinite light down there. There's no expression of any source of anything at all. Up here, everything is just bubbling with expression of its source in a higher realm. Down there, everything just seems to say, "Here I am and here I was, and that's what I am."

Michael: That's precisely it! That is the Ultimate Revelation of the Essence of the Infinite Light!

Raphael: It is?

Michael: Yes! Because that little script they seem to say—that's really the voice of the Essence of Being, that says, "Here I am and here I was, and I am that which I will be." In our spiritual realms we can only imagine such things. There, it's a tangible first-hand experience!

Gabriel: So they've got this Absolutely Infinite Light down in that dark, dingy material realm, and we can't tap into it without them.

Michael: Now you're beginning to see the urgency of the situation. Time is running out. They need to be connected to their source up here to continue their existence. At present, they endure on a sort of "initial subscriber free plan." But that can only last maybe a few hours more. If we don't connect them soon, by giving them names according to their supernal connections up here, they'll just fade back into the void.

Raphael: And then, never again any of that fabulous sensation.

Gabriel: Nothing but the same, regulated ration of divine flow every day for an eternity.

Michael: It might not be even that. The Boss may just decide to scrap the whole thing. What's the point, with no excitement or novelty involved.

Raphael: Alright! Alright! I've heard enough! Send the Supernal Ox down! Just don't let me watch what happens to him!

Gabriel: I'm making the adjustments right now, just look in the projection capsule display. He's morphing down and down through each of the progressively lower spiritual realms. Passing through Creation Realms, now to the realms of Formation, into the worlds of Action. Ok, now he'll be making that quantum leap into physicality. I'll need to enter the secret code granted for this operation.

Michael: Gevald! Gabe, you did it! He looks just like the original beast in question!

Raphael: Don't tell me! Don't make me look!

Michael: And he's standing right next to him! Now he just has to name the thing!

Gabriel: We'll open up lines of communication now. ShOR! Can you read me, ShOR?!

ShOR: <grunt>. [apparently oblivious, starts munching the grass.]

Gabriel: I'll amplify the signal. Obviously, the descent has dulled his signal perceptions further than I had estimated.

ShOR! STOP MUNCHING THE GREEN STUFF AND CONFIRM RECEIPT OF SIGNAL!!!

ShOR: {Shakes head]. <GRUNT>

Gabriel: That seems to be the sign he's received the signal. Now if we can remind him of his mission. ShOR! LOOK AT THE BEAST TO YOUR LEFT AND CALL IT BY NAME!!!

ShOR: [Looks to left. Notices another ox eating grass.]

Gabriel: Yes! He's got the message! He's pondering the other ox!

ShOR: [Looks back at his own grass, and then back at the other ox's grass.]

Gabriel: ...And he's realized that he and that other beast share a commonality. Now, certainly, he'll be able to draw into it his own name directly from the Supernal Chariot of the heavenly spheres! ShOR! NAME IT NOW!

ShOR: MOOOO! [clunks over to the other ox, pushes him aside and munches on his grass]. <grunt.>

Michael: He's almost humanlike.

Gabriel: Yes, that's the problem, I think he's descended too far. He's lost the capacity for coherent speech. Can't name anything without that.

Raphael: No wonder he's experiencing such frustration and anxiety! Can't you have some mercy on the poor creature and allow it to retain some intelligent and communicative features while descending into the physical realm?

Gabriel: Ok, here are some minor adjustments. Now this beast-angel will be capable of speech and conscious thought. Let's play that again.

ShOR! WHAT IS THE NAME OF THAT OX YOU JUST SHOVED INTO THE DITCH??!!

ShOR: [Looks into ditch, ponders, then answers] "Subdued competitor." Can I get back to the green stuff now?

Gabriel: That's not a Name! That's an ego-relational designation!

Raphael: Yes. He's become entirely ego-centered. It's so pitiful. You must rescue him fast!

Michael: Gabe, Raphael's right. The whole thing is hopeless. This little experiment we've done has only gone to prove that which we should have known all along. It just can't be done.

Gabriel: Of course it can't be done. It's an auto-conflicting task! It's downright recursive, that's what it is!

Raphael: Why is that?

Gabriel: Because you can't descend below and remain above at the same time! And you can't be a something 100%, like they are down there, and get inside something else at the same time! And—most important—you can't look at something physical and see anything spiritual about it all at once! And all those three things are precisely what we are demanding this ox to do!

Raphael: But maybe...

Michael: Raphael, look at the evidence. When the ShOR from the Supernal Chariot descended below, did he retain any spiritual qualities? No, he became exactly where sent him to—physical. He couldn't remain above at the same time as going below. Of course not—it doesn't make any sense!

Gabriel: And when he looked at the other beast, he couldn't see it for what it was—only how it relates to him. He couldn't be himself and get out of himself all at once. I mean, it's just ridiculous. How could we have imagined that to begin with?

Michael: And this preposterous idea of being able to perceive spiritual energy within a physical being—well you obviously can't see both at once! They're so, just—contradictory!

Gabriel, Raphael, I hate to say this, but we might as well just close up shop right now and forget the whole thing. I mean, it was a nice experiment, but...

Gabriel: You mean, we've lost?

Michael: All is lost. It's over before it even started. We've just got to close up and...

[Theatre lights go off, audience is leaving. Maintenance angels enter to close up shop.]

Raphael: Hold on! Which experiment do you mean?

130

Michael: The whole thing. The cosmos. Upper ones. Lower Ones. 3D ones, 4D ones, 5D ones—all the way up to our own, and even higher, to the initial emanations that broke through the Great Void and before. If that lowest of all low worlds can't be connected, there's just no point. You can't imagine how dull it could be...

[Maintenance angels are walking in and out with stepladders, etc..]

Raphael: But the Boss said that this Adam...

Gabriel: Are you still banking on that? But we just explained that it's totally impossible?

Raphael: But it must be so! The Boss set up this match didn't He?

[Below, Adam, who has been joyously discovering his world, stumbles across the ox]

Michael: But Gabriel and I just finished explaining to you that it's impossible.

[Adam is happily examining the ox from all angles. Then he starts imitating it.]

Gabriel: Yeah, he'll probably just look at it and call it "hamburgers" or some such ego-relational designation.

Raphael: But, maybe we should just give him a chance?

[Adam is stroking the ox.]

Gabriel: Chance? What's the point of chance? If you know something just isn't, then it isn't, right? I mean, we are intellectual beings up here. There aren't any greater intellects around. And our logic says it just can't be.

[Adam has made friends with the ox and is now riding gleefully on its back. Maintenance angels are unscrewing light bulbs and taking the cosmos apart.]

Raphael: Just give him a try! Just to be fair! Who knows? Maybe he can do it!

Michael: Raphael, listen to common sense. For any creature to be able to do such a thing, he would have to be full of such contradictory elements as to oppose the basic laws of logic themselves.

Now, we know the whole order of things is based on that logic...

Gabriel: So it's impossible! PERIOD. IT DEFIES THE WHOLE BASIS OF THE ENTIRE COSMOS OPERATING SYSTEM! IT'S...IT'S...

Michael: Illogical!

Gabriel: INCONCEIVABLE!

Michael: And Unachievable!

Adam: SHOR!

Michael, Gabriel & Raphael: WHAT??!!

Adam: [Pleasantly] Yes, I think it would be nice to call you ShOR.

Ox: MMMMMMMMMOOOOOOOOOOOOOOOOOO!

[the Moo travels upward, lighting up a chain of angels in blinding light, until reaching the Supernal Chariot which is charged with flying sparks and crackling, high-voltage sound effects as the Supernal Ox makes the connection with its transcendent Source. The angels all raise their voices in heavenly praise, rising higher and higher in pitch and volume as Michael, Gabriel and Raphael prostrate themselves in complete nullification to the Ultimate Boss of All Things.]

Adam: [Now viewing a donkey] And this one, this one I would like to call "Chamor." [Repeat heavenly scene]

Adam: [Repeats animal after animal and bird and insect all to the tune of the heavenly choir.]

Adam: And now, about myself, I suppose my Creator wishes that I should name myself too. So I will call myself Adam.

Angels: Hallelu!!!

Adam: Because I was formed from the earth, which is called "Adama."

Voice from Heaven: And also, Adam, because you are similar (domeh) to the Infinite Light Above, which knows no boundaries. Yes, you were formed from the earth, but your soul is of the essence of G–d, and in you the two are fused. You—unlike the angels—can traverse the boundaries that separate soul from body, spirit from matter, heaven from earth. You alone can look at a physical beast and see spiritual life and beauty. You alone can make this world of yours a place where I am revealed.

And what, then shall you call Me?

Adam: [Scratching his head and pondering] You are Who You Are and What You Are. You are beyond all names!

Voice: But nevertheless, give me a name that my creatures should call upon Me, and they shall be bonded to Me from their own subjective experience as well. And then I shall dwell in this world I have made.

Adam: Very well, then I shall name You. You it is proper to call _____, because You are the Master [Adon] over all Your creations.

Angels: Hallelu!!! Hallelu!!! Hallelu!!!

Part IV: Backstage

Host: *Listen, Mr. Angel, before we pack that thing up, could I just ask one more question of those little guys?*

Angel: Okay, well let's start it up again…

Host: *And make sure they have that consciousness setting on.*

Angel: For recursive self-awareness?

Host: *If that's what you call it.*

Angel: So here. I've set the parameters—a little more enlightenment this time. You start it up yourself.

Host: *Wow. Now there's that little guy again. Hey, little guy!*

Little Guy: I hear a voice. The mighty lord speaks unto me.

Host: *Hey, nice to see you again!*

LG: Behold, O Mighty One, your faithful servant awaits his command!

Host: *So you remember who I am?*

LG: You are the Great Voice in the Sky.

Host: *Sounds good.*

LG: The Most Wise and Powerful.

Host: *Hey, you're a lot more fun to have around than this know-it-all angel wise-guy.*

LG: Manipulator of Heaven and Earth! And I am your lowly and humble servant.

Host: *Of course. After all, I created your entire world.*

LG: Out of the formless muck.

Host: *Try "out of a black switch-box."*

LG: Out of the blackness of swish wash.

Host: *Not swish-wash! Black box! It's got dials and buttons and checkboxes—I set the parameters for every detail of your world down there!*

LG: You are the god over all other gods! The god of water and the god of fire, the god of gravity and the god of electromagnetism, behold they all bow down before you.

Host: *Oh, really. I thought I just turn the dials and set those parameters. In fact, I generate you out of the void, as well.*

LG: Oh, me you don't generate out of the void.

Host: *Now what makes you think that?*

LG: O Great Master with Big Voice, all is but an illusion before your true oneness. All is but vanity and poofy dust. All is false imagination.

Host: *Including you, little guy.*

LG: No, I am for real. For I am conscious of my world about me. I am conscious of my own being. I am me.

Host: *Oh, the I. The recursive self-awareness thing. We just set that as one of the parameters. I think it's this dial, here.. With self-awareness, you can be my faithful servant and I can give you commands. You can decide, "Should I do this or should I rebel?" And when you decide to follow commands, it's just soooo much more thrilling.*

          That's what makes this whole world-making contraption so spiffy ——your sense of "I" that we programmed. Without that, it would be just another 3D video RPG.

          See, we could even turn it down and you will...

LG: No! You mustn't do that!

Host: *Hey, I could even make you disappear altogether...*

LG: Scientist! The Big Voice in Sky has been angered and threatens us with frontal lobotomy! We must escape! Who knows? He may force REBOOT!

Scientist: Don't worry, I have found a back door to another world-system. We can back ourselves up and re-download when he calms down.

Host: *Angel, this is awesome. We've got to market this...*

Sources: See Likutei Sichos, vol. 15, pp. 13-19

THE MENORA FILES

Reason vs. Paradox

Light 1: The Contract

─────Begin Forwarded Message ─────

Subject: Contract Tender, Menora Miracle

```
Date:      Kislev 25 3:29:15.036 PM

From:    miracles@admin.hvn

To:      MiraclesRUs@engineering.hvn,
         QualityMiracles@engineering.hvn,
         OutaNowhere@engineering.hvn,
         FlamingWonders@engineering.hvn,
         MikesMiracleShop@engineering.hvn,
         MiraclesUnlimited@engineering.hvn,
         SeaSplitters@engineering.hvn,
         MadeInHeaven@engineering.hvn,
         PhysicsBusters@engineering.hvn
```

Background: In direct consequence to the overwhelming success of the Maccabee project and as a sign of appreciation to the courageous Maccabees who made that success possible, the administration of Heaven Inc. has decided to provide yet another wondrous manifestation of the truth behind the cosmos, a.k.a. a miracle.

As is well known, the Maccabees yesterday regained control of the Holy Temple in Jerusalem from the Greek Army, and spent most of today sweeping away the broken beer bottles and associated mess. In answer to the sincere search of the Maccabees for ritually appropriate Menora oil, Heaven engaged the services of Hidden Surprises Inc., who were successful in engineering yet another miracle, the discovery of a flask of pure olive oil hidden in the ground and sealed with the seal of the High Priest.

Now, another miracle is needed. The flask discovered contains only one day's worth of oil. Although it will take eight days to prepare new olive oil, nevertheless, the Maccabees have decided to go ahead and use this oil immediately. In response to this inspiring display of alacrity, zeal and devotion, the administration has been instructed to perform one more miracle and ensure that this oil will burn for all eight days.

We are presently accepting proposals on the implementation of this miracle. All applicants should prepare a detailed description of the mechanics of their proposed implementation, as well as their qualifications to perform such services.

Note that requirements surrounding this miracle are quite stringent:

1. Eight Days: All applicants must demonstrate that their proposal will not just burn for eight days, but also provide a miracle on each of the eight days. Since the flask found by the Maccabees already contains enough oil for one day to begin with, some creativity will be necessary to provide this effect.

2. Fair Compensation: In consonance with a long-standing policy on all heavenly matters, often known as the "measure-for-measure" policy, the miracle should reflect the attitude and acts to which it is resultant. Applicants should ensure the proposal blends smoothly with the general theme of the Maccabee vs. Hellenist episode and the no-compromise strategy of the Maccabees.

3. Halacha: At least the fundaments of halachic requirements for the Menora of the Holy Temple must be taken into consideration, with extra points for fulfilling all requirements, and bonus points for extra-compulsory details.

Please submit your proposals and all correspondence to this address. Adjudication of presentations by all bidders will commence today at 3:29:15.536 PM. AV equipment for presentations will be provided by Heaven Inc.

————— End Forwarded Message ———

Light 11: The Consultant

The scene up there is far beyond the capacity of our earthly imaginations, since we imagine everything in coarse material terms. Perhaps I can attempt to explain it in whatever terms we share, as long as you promise to keep in mind that in truth, it is something far abstracted from any of what I might say.

On the appointed day, an angel of wisdom, known as a "maggid", stood in still reverence, waiting for the assembly to be called to order.

His eyes scanned the 70 members of the Heavenly Supreme Court. They stood (nobody sits up there—it's just not in the repertoire) at a semi-oblong table, allowing all to see one another. But the central position of this table is not locatable, beyond dimension or place, since it is the (un)space of The Chief Magistrate of All Things.

To the right hand of The Chief stood the ChairAngel (a.k.a., "Av Beit Din"), a powerful radiance about his face and magnificent robes flowing down from his shoulders. To the left stood the next wisest of the angels and from that point on, in either direction, the remainder of the esteemed judges stood solemnly by rank in G–dly wisdom.

On cue, the maggid made his case.

"My lords, esteemed masters of justice and righteousness," he spoke, moving his hands gracefully, "Today you convene to discuss a matter of serious, practical implications for every generation of the Jewish people from now unto eternity. Indeed, whereas the lights of other festivals may at times of darkness be all but extinguished, and eventually are destined to be entirely absorbed within the great light of the World to Come, the lights of Chanukah are constant and eternal—as per the talmudic gloss of Nachmanides and his commentary to parshat Behalotecha."

"We are well aware of the gravity of our meeting today," patiently interjected the ChairAngel. "Is there anything in particular you feel has not been taken into account in our planned adjudication?"

The eyes of the maggid widened. "As you know, I am the maggid appointed to instruct an illustrious student, one by whose light all the Community of Israel shall proceed through the thick darkness of the last leg of their exile until the final redemption. He is none other than Yosef Karo, illustrious author of the Beit Yosef as well as the Shulchan Aruch, the most authoritative code of Jewish Law."

Angels are an excitable group. At the mention of that holy name, heartbeats accelerated, ethereal wings began to flutter and amidst the scattered exclamations of "Yosef Karo!", "the Beit Yosef!", a spontaneous chorus of audio-oriented beings burst into harmonious accolades of praise and appellations upon the aforementioned.

Eventually, the court was called to order.

"My illustrious student," continued the maggid, "will write about the very issue we are gathered here today to discuss in his halachic gloss, Beit Yosef—"the House of Yosef". Indeed, the matter will from that time on be known by his name, 'the Difficulty Posed By the Beit Yosef'. It is only appropriate therefore, that he be invited to sit in on our proceedings as an outside consultant."

The ChairAngel scanned quickly the faces of the assembled heavenly judges, noting their unanimous approval. "Clerk!" he called, "Bring us Yosef Karo!"

The clerk looked back, bewildered. "But, your honor, Yosef Karo does not live for the better part of another two millennia!"

144

"Bring us Yosef Karo," the ChairAngel commanded firmly. "This is heaven. And we need him now."

An Angel of Sympathy who stood near the clerk's post read his confused face, leaned over and whispered, "If we don't consult with him now, eventually we're going to have to retro-write history according to his decision anyway."

The clerk shrugged and walked out the door, still shaking his head. But he was back in no time. Trumpets blasted in royal fanfare and drums rolled as the entrance of Yosef Karo, was announced. The entire heavenly court rose in awe and glowed in neon colors. The vocal ensemble once again joined together in celestial chorus.

Then he entered. In jeweled turban and flowing robes, his piercing eyes shining like sapphires, he walked forth in all humility, yet with the elegance and majesty of a mighty king. A heavenly court clerk rushed him a portfolio and a nametag and led him to his place at the consultant's desk.

The proceedings commenced.

Light III: Quality

Quality Miracles is known for their high-end, lavish presentations. This one was no let-down. The upbeat, surround-sound music came on, the lights dimmed, and in a sprinkle of sparks, a sales associate dramatically appeared at stage center cupping in his hands a small golden unlit lamp.

"Brother angels, behold with your eyes!"

His hands opened and the lamp came in full view of all the court. The enlightened beings gasped in unison.

"Yes, you all recall! It is the holy lamp that was lit by those most transcendent and magnificent of beings, the Matriarchs of the Souls of Israel, Sarah and Rivka!"

Now the 3D video came on. The image of Sarah leaning her shining countenance of beauty over the Shabbat lamp in the pre-twilight of the Negev brought tears to the eyes of the Angels of Sensitivity. The hearts of the most judgmental beings were captured as, with breathtaking focus and inspiration, she uttered the words as though counting golden coins,

"Blessed are You, _____ our All-Pervasive Force, Master of the Cosmos, Who has made us wholly transcendent through His mitzvahs and enjoined us to light the lamp of the Holy Shabbos."

Then, as she waved gently her hands over the flame, serene light flashed out in all directions, illuminating upper and lower worlds.

"And so," the agent from Quality continued, "you must remember the great and wondrous miracle that occurred then, how the Natural Order of Things was transcended so the pure light of this magnificent being could illuminate all the worlds for an entire week, every week, for her entire life, and for the life of her heiress Rivka, as well! To this day, that miracle empowers every Jewish woman and girl to light up her world just the same!"

In a brilliant twist of suspense, the music found its way to a sudden silence, the video halted on a still frame. "And who engineered that miracle?" The sales rep's voice echoed through the marble hall.

With eye-riveting form, the still image morphed into the logo of "Quality Miracles" as the multitude of high-res amplifiers burst forth with "Quality! Quality Miracles! The natural solution to all your miracle needs!"

The music ended on a sharp climax, the video faded away, and the crowd burst into applause as the lights came back up.

The Quality Miracles VP of Development strutted forth. Riding on the excitement in the air, he began promptly. "Of course, the Chanukah Miracle project presents certain features that were not present in the Sarah and Rebecca scenario. We've noted the two most significant: The Sarah and Rebecca lamp only burnt for seven days—this miracle must occur for eight. Secondly, the Shabbat Lamp was a single miracle spread over an extended duration of time, whereas, in our case the Menora must be rekindled every afternoon, thereby providing eight distinct miracles."

The wise members of the court stroked their silvery beards and nodded their heads in heedfulness. Rabbi Yosef Karo only stared intently, as though chewing into every word.

"We believe our previous implementation can be easily extended to fill these requirements. And now, here is our senior engineer for an explanation of the technology behind this amazing accomplishment."

A complex chart appeared at the presenter's position as the senior engineer stepped forward. It was one of those charts that only an angel could read, describing in multiple dimensions the links and chains that serve as the backbone of created entities.

"Over here," the engineer pointed, "we see the letters, or combination of forces that form the word 'shemen'—meaning 'oil'. This connects with the Divine source of olives, as we see in this link, here. Note the intimate connection with the sphere of Wisdom of the World of Emanation, which is preserved throughout the creative process. As this linkage descends below, olive oil is manifested in each of the worlds, in each according to the parameters of that world. Finally, as it descends into the lowest world, the 'World of Action and Physicality', it becomes an actual material substance, derived by the crushing or squeezing of physical olives."

"As you are well aware, most miracles are performed by invasive fiddling with the mechanics of such links and letter combinations. Turning water to blood, dust into lice, vinegar into oil are all examples of such 'rearrangements' of the system."

"Our strategy is far less invasive: You'll notice there is quite a bit of leeway in the *quality* dimension of this particular linkage. This explains why every olive produces its own quality of oil, with a wide margin of variety, especially in combustibility. Our technique is to hyper-extend that quality margin, thereby manifesting in the target olive oil down there an enormous capacity to burn—even to eight times the original average power."

It was obvious the judges were impressed with the professionalism, thoroughness and high entertainment value of the presentation. Heads turned towards each other, sharing comments and nods of approval. The VP of Development strutted back on stage and opened the floor to questions.

Yosef Karo alone appeared unmoved. He looked about him, shook his head almost with disdain, and spoke assertively at the VP. "Being from a practical world, where nitty-gritty details matter, I am still unclear on your proposal."

The engineer got out his charts again, preparing to explain things in greater depth.

"No, I don't mean your schematics, or your software code or any of that. I'm talking about the human interface. How does this actually get implemented?"

The Quality Team members looked a bit shaken. They were experts in high tech solutions. Humans were a necessary component in implementation, but not one that got a lot of attention.

"To be specific," continued Yosef Karo, "what exactly are the Maccabees supposed to do with this oil on the first afternoon they light it?"

"Well," answered the VP slowly and cautiously as though sensing a trap, "They put the oil in the cups of the Menora, like they always used to do, and they light it."

"And how much oil do they put in?"

The engineer jumped in. "One eighth! Why should they put in any more? They only need one eighth, so that's how much they'll put in!"

Now one of the judges took a stab. "But how are they supposed to know that one eighth is going to last through the entire night?"

The VP was struggling to hold his cool as murmurs were heard throughout the assembly. An employee rushed up to whisper something in his ear. "Yes, we've taken that into consideration," he continued. "There's a contingency allowance to sub-contract Echo

Communications, a firm that deals in supplying earthly beings with minor levels of prophecy, sometimes known as 'Ruach Hakodesh'. You'll find that clause on page..."

The employee who had done the whispering could no longer contain himself and interjected, "Actually, they'll probably figure it out on their own. They'll say, look, if the Almighty only gave us one flask of pure oil and of course He knows we can't get any replacement for eight days, it must be this is super-eight powered oil."

Most of the judges were not impressed with this response, being rather skeptical of the mental capacity of most earthly beings. The VP glanced over his shoulder at his employee with a biting cold stare, then turned back to his audience swiftly donning a warm smile. "By the way," he noted, "you'll observe that with this solution there is a separate miracle each of the eight days. Each night only a little bit of oil burns an entire night. Every night a new miracle, for eight nights just as the contract tender required."

"The eight days is just wonderful and some minor prophecy is fine with me." The voice of Yosef Karo broke through the confusion, commanding silence. "I have a different problem with your solution." The VP's neck was outstretched as Yosef Karo continued.

"As you know, the Torah does not state a precise quantity of oil to be placed in the Menora for each lighting, only that there should be enough to last for the longest nights of the winter. Our sages determined this amount to be a little over six fluid ounces. Just so happens, that's the amount found in that little flask down there. Which means, they're going to have to put the whole thing in."

"Aha," the ChairAngel spoke now, "that would be true in general, but here, remember, with this oil, one eighth is the appropriate amount for the longest nights of the winter! On the contrary, putting more would mean a violation of the halacha you just cited!"

"With all due respect to his honored chair, I've yet to finish," continued Yosef Karo, calmly, "There is another halacha that applies to all the vessels in the Holy Temple. Out of respect for their sanctity, whenever they are filled they must be filled entirely."

The VP beamed, oblivious to the trap laid for him. "So we will have them fill the entire thing the first night! And then, only an eighth will burn the first night, another eighth the second..."

Karo pounced like a tiger. "But didn't the ChairAngel just declare that to be a violation of the halacha!!! You'll have eight times the established amount the first night, seven times on the second, and so on."

The hall burst into an uproar of debate. The brilliant counter-offence of Yosef Karo had the entire heavenly court ignited. With Quality's solution there seemed no way out: You could fulfill one requirement or the other —but there was no way to fulfill both.

Above the confusion, another judge yelled out, "Filling the vessel to the brim is an non-compulsory requirement! Let them fill up only an eighth, since that's all they can do!"

"First of all," Yosef Karo replied, commanding immediate silence, "the whole thing is non-compulsory to begin with. The Maccabees really could light with impure oil. When the entire community is in a state of impurity, such as they are after a war, impure offerings are permitted as per the Babylonian Talmud, Pesachim, folio 80a.."

"So what's the whole deal with this contract tender for a miracle?!" The VP waved a paper in exasperation.

"Think for a minute," Karo reasoned. "Why did they search so hard for ritually pure oil when they could have used any old oil given the circumstances? And why did the Almighty contract the previous miracle of providing a hidden, untouched flask? Wasn't it all in order that they should perform the Menora lighting in the most perfect way, not just 'so-so and get it over with'?"

"And that is the job of Heaven Inc.," he declared. "To perform a miracle that allows the Maccabees to go beyond the letter of the law, as they have committed themselves to do, for the sake of the eternity of the Jewish Nation!"

The judges were enthralled with the insights of Yosef Karo. Fascinated, they took in every word.

Lowering his voice mischievously, Karo continued. "Furthermore, who says they are allowed to fill the Menora only partially each day, when they could fill it to the brim?"

The VP from Quality timidly ventured, "And with what will they fill it to the brim each day if they only have one flask?"

"With impure oil!!" shot back Yosef Karo. "Since that is perfectly permissible under these conditions."

The entire court exploded into animated debate, reviewing, shaking their heads and waving their wings frantically. Once again, the ChairAngel called for order.

"I humbly propose," he advised his colleagues, "we consider another proposal."

Light IV: Quantity

Official Report Card: Quality Miracles Proposal.

Pros:

- Excellent multimedia presentation, esp. audio effects.

- Provides a miracle for each of the eight days.

- Elegance: Supernatural miracle produced without disturbing the natural order.

- Fulfills most halachic requirements, such as use of authentic olive oil and natural burning of oil to produce flame.

Cons:

- Lack of coordination between team members.

- Actual implementation not well conceived. Little consideration given to human interface issues.

- One major halachic concern: The Menora regulations require that precisely the amount of oil to burn through one winter night be placed in the cups of the Menora. It is also preferable that the cups all be completely filled. With Quality's proposal, there is no way both these conditions can be mutually fulfilled. It has even been proposed that, under such conditions, the use of impure oil in proper quantities would be preferable over using the limited amount of pure oil that was miraculously discovered.

Rating: 3.5 wings

The man from OutaNowhere appeared from out of nowhere pushing a trolley cart with coffee and Danishes. "Your esteemed judges have been having an intense session here," he announced. "Let's all take a break for refreshments!"

The judges noticed coffee mugs on their desks. The sales rep held only a tiny coffeepot, but proceeded to fill cup after cup with heavenly coffee—not stopping for a single refill.

Continuing to pour, he started his spiel: "Yes, esteemed judges, I'm sure you'll agree we've got a supernatural, nifty technology here. But don't imagine this is some useless gimmick! As a matter of fact, OutaNowhere technology was originally developed to fulfill a **real need**. To fill you in on the history of our product, just listen to this testimonial from our first successful client, none other than the prophet, Elisha!"

All eyes turned to the 3D video display, now filled with the scene of a quiet corner in the Garden of Eden. Sitting on a thatch chair, an agent of OutaNowhere was interviewing Elisha who sat across the coffee table from her.

> "Elisha, you are well known for your compassion and wonderful acts of kindness in the earthly realm. Much of your good work was possible due to your ability to transcend the present tense and see matters from a higher time-definition. You also developed an amazing and unique repertoire of record-breaking miracles. But there was one time you turned to OutaNowhere technologies for assistance. Why?"
>
> "Truthfully, everything I know I received from my teacher, Elijah. But then came a very difficult case, a woman whose husband had been a member in good standing of the

Professional Prophet's Association until his premature passing. The poor woman was left with two little boys to support, no pension, no real source of income. Neither her landlord nor the rental board had any sympathy. By the time she came to me, she had in her hand a notice that if she didn't pay the rent fast, her two boys would be seized as payment!"

"That's horrifying! But couldn't you just co-sign on a long term loan or something?"

"That wouldn't be professional. I'm a prophet. My job is to help people discover their own inner wealth, not breed dependence, as you suggest. So I followed standard case analysis technique and asked the lady to describe her assets."

"Which were two boys..."

"Which I understood as a reflection of the love and sense of awe within her. This, however, was apparently in real danger—as reflected by the collection notice mentioned earlier."

"So all these material concerns and details were all merely reflections of a higher, spiritual drama?"

"You're with me now. She also had a small flask of olive oil, reflecting her essential spiritual self. I needed some way for this inner spiritual wealth to release itself to the point of becoming manifest in her earthly domain."

"Now, how could you do that?"

"Well, that's when I remembered a business card I had been handed just the day before, while wandering about the higher spheres. I checked my pocket, and there it was, 'OutaNowhere Technologies Inc.'."

"Was OutaNowhere responsive when you needed them?"

"Their tech support was fantastic. Immediately, we put together a plan whereby all the lady had to do was visit her neighbors and borrow their jugs, pots, pans—any types of physical-realm vessels and containers. We realized this was basically what she was missing—tangible, practical ways to express her inner soul. She gathered all this stuff in her house, closed the doors, let down the blinds and then started filling everything up with her little flask of oil."

"That must have been an exciting scene."

"It certainly was. The little boys were running back and forth, back and forth, bringing containers and more containers, while the oil just kept pouring and pouring out of the flask. Finally, she asked for one more pot and her boys told her there wasn't a single one left. And neither was there any more oil."

"And what happened to that nefarious landlord?"

"With sales from the oil, she was able to pay him off, with enough left over that she could just live off the interest."

"So, thanks to support from OutaNowhere, another great act of compassion was accomplished in the physical realm."

"Not only that. This episode was reported and discussed in all the major prophetic journals. It was recorded as a classic for all times in the Book of Kings. You see, it wasn't just that lady who was helped. Since that time, anyone that is in a dire state of spiritual poverty is able to overcome his or her situation by doing the same as she did—but in spiritual terms. By temporarily ignoring their state of spiritual poverty and just collecting vessels of mitzvahs and acts of kindness and allowing that essential self to pour into them, unlimited—eventually all those deficiencies are spontaneously overcome. I'll challenge everyone in our audience to just try it out and see."

"And that message to the world is all thanks to OutaNowhere."

"That's right. Like another cup of coffee?"

The shot of Elisha pouring a cup of coffee for his host spun out to make way for an animated "OutaNowhere" logo, accompanied by a snappy "OutaNowhere—there when you need us" jingle.

As the judges were sipping their heavenly coffee, Yosef Karo was busy taking notes. Once in a while, he stopped to shake his head. It was obvious something about the presentation was bothering him.

Light V: Prozac

OutaNowhere had learned their lesson from what had occurred with Quality. You could tell that from their presentation.

"We're not going to bore you with all the technical details behind this tremendous feat of spiritual engineering," continued the sales rep. "After all, we're an end-user oriented company. We've put a lot of thought into the practical, nitty-gritty —the things that count in the physical world where our target user resides. Here's our *human interface expert* to discuss ground level implementation."

The HI expert stepped up in front of the 3D-video display area. "Actually, we've got two options to present. The first option you've seen a demo of already, but here's a short animation that will demonstrate how far we've gone into the details. You'll also observe the virtual model of the Temple Menora here next to me."

A life-size image of a Hasmonean Cohen holding a jug of olive oil in front of the Menora appeared. This being heaven, with more than 3 dimensions available, the image displayed that the jug was full.

"Here's the initial state. Now observe what happens as the Cohen fills the cups of the Menora on the first day."

As the Cohen filled each cup, the jug became successively emptier. But then, just before the last drop poured out, the flask suddenly refilled itself. The Cohen froze for a moment, puzzled, stared into the jug, and then ran out of the Holy Chamber yelling, "A MIRACLE! A MIRACLE!"

"Note," the HI expert commented, "that as this scenario occurs each of the eight days, we have in effect eight separate miracles. This is in direct contradistinction to certain other solutions that offer only one miraculous state-change of the olive oil, which then remains consistent over the next eight days. Obviously, you can see the superiority of our..."

"You call that superiority!?" yelled a snide voice from the back of the room. It was the VP from Quality. All this time he had been sitting in a back row, arms folded, waiting for his chance to jump back into the ring. Now, completely out of protocol, unable to contain himself any longer, he grabbed it.

"Why, with your solution, the only ones who ever see a miracle are those who are there at the time of the lighting! After that, it's just everyday burning of olive oil. Our solution provides any witness at any point in time a clear view of a miraculous state, every day, at every moment!"

"But you must agree," replied the OutaNowhere expert, smugly, "that the actual miracle only occurs once in your solution. Once your oil is set to its high quality level on the first day, it just remains there. Here, every day, a miracle must occur for new oil to appear!"

"What does that have to do with the project requirements?" shot back Quality's VP.

The Chair Angel called for order, chiding Quality's VP for his disruption of protocol. But the HI expert was delighted his competition had provided the opportunity for him to fully present his thesis.

"The success of a miracle," he explained, "must be measured by the end user experience. Consider here the impact upon the human psyche. A continuous state of miracle would become accepted as natural routine within a single day. The sense of wonderment would rapidly wear out. By calling for spaced, intermittent miracles, we hope to sustain the wonderment factor for a much longer period. This, after a careful study of human psychology..."

"Psychology shmykology!" shot back the Quality VP. "Who are you kidding? What do you know about human psychology? What do any of us know? We're angels, for heaven's sake!"

"That's right," replied the expert. "We were on the design team."

"Design team!? Design team!?" mocked the VP. "Haven't you read the Adam Files?! If it were up to us, the Earthly Human Project would never have gotten beyond the World of Emanation stage!!"

The judges were enjoying the entertainment, but the ChairAngel finally had to interfere. "We have a human subject right here," he remarked. "Why don't we ask him?"

Rabbi Karo was reluctant. "I believe your test would be more meaningful if performed on a more skeptical specimen," he suggested. "Perhaps you have a Hellenist about here somewhere? Or maybe even an authentic ancient Greek?"

"Your honor," ventured one of the lesser judges. "Perhaps we could call in the Sar Shel Yavan?"

The ChairAngel's face glowed with delight, as did the faces of the others. "Yes!" they cried out, one to the other. "The Sar Shel Yavan! Who else could we call to test end user experience?"

In the data processing protocol of heaven, there are only seventy nations. Over each of these is appointed a "sar" or "officer", somewhat lower than a full-fledged angel. "Yavan" is the name by which the ancient Greeks are known. Thus the "Sar Shel Yavan" —the officer appointed over ancient Greece.

He came hobbling on crutches, covered with wounds of war. His substance was as the walls of the chamber, that heavenly version of marble. You could still see the beauty and gracefulness for which he had been known, but military defeat and shame had taken its toll.

We won't get into the details of the user testing, at least in this edition. Suffice it to mention that the Sar refused to acknowledge any miracles, attributing everything to natural causes. When pressed, he began to accuse all the heavenly court of being "no better than those superstitious Jews, believing in things that make no sense, relying on empirical evidence rather than the truth of the natural sciences."

At any rate, he stayed to audit the rest of the hearings.

"Truthfully," the ChairAngel commented to Yosef Karo, "We've never had much success with end user experience. On occasion, we went through ten iterations of miracles before achieving our goals—and even then only with partial success."

The other judges nodded, resignedly.

"We even," the Chair Angel hesitated, "had to...drown the test subjects at the end of that procedure...to cover up the data."

Yosef Karo took over. "However, I would like to go back to the scenario presented in your detailed animation," he continued. The OutaNowhere expert was relieved, feeling he was back on a more solid cloud.

"On the first day, that is the afternoon of the 25th, a miracle occurs, correct?"

"A very startling miracle, your honor. At least, certainly to the Maccabees for whom it is performed."

"And on the second day, the afternoon of the 26th, the same miracle?"

"That's correct."

"And so on, all the way until the eighth afternoon?"

"Precisely."

"And then what happens?"

"On the ninth?"

"No, on the eighth. What miracle occurs on the eighth? Remember, there are eight days of Chanukah. Or are you proposing to change that?"

"Well, just the same as the seven days before could occur." The human interface expert passed a quick, nervous glance over to the other members of his team.

"I'm sorry," countered the ChairAngel. "But we have a policy concerning such matters. Miracles must always serve a practical function. Nobody, not even Heaven Inc., is allowed to make miracles just for the heck of it. And in this case, since new oil will be arriving on the ninth day anyway, there is no need for your miracle on the eighth. The Cohen can just empty out his entire jug on the eighth day, with no need for your miraculous auto-refill out of nowhere."

The sales rep from OutaNowhere was motioning wildly to the HI expert. All those dealings with earthly beings had dulled his angelic intellectual brilliance. But finally the puzzled expression on the expert's face resolved into glee, as he exclaimed, "Yes! Oh yes! That's why we have solution #2. Here it goes:"

Another animation began. The initial state was the same, but this time, the jug emptied entirely. The animation collapsed the next 12 hours into a few nanoseconds, during which the oil progressively decreased in quantity. Then, just as it hit the last drop, oil returned suddenly to the cups of the Menora. A Hasmonean Cohen entered the Holy Chamber that morning —technically day two of Chanukah —to prepare the Menora as per Temple ritual. He looked in the cups, saw the oil and ran out waving his arms and yelling, "A MIRACLE! A MIRACLE!"

"Now, you'll observe in this scenario," concluded the expert, "since the miracle occurs the day after, instead of immediately, the miracle must also therefore occur on the 8th day of Chanukah, in order that the Menora may be lit on that afternoon!"

"You'll also notice," pitched in the sales rep, "that we've provided all of you with auto-refilling coffee mugs to demonstrate this wonderful application of our technology. We're not limited to refilling the source —we can even cause the recipient vessel to auto-refill!"

Yosef Karo sat poker-faced, astonished by the trap OutaNowhere had laid for itself. "And what about the first day?" he softly queried.

"The first day?"

"Yes. You said the miracle doesn't occur until the day after. What miracle do we celebrate on the first day then?"

The expert was by now searching his pockets for his Prozac™. His team members had their heads practically between their knees. The CEO of OutaNowhere could no longer take it. He jumped up there in a last ditch attempt to save his company.

"Gentle Angels," he said, feigning suave and good humor. "I'm sure you yourselves have realized the most obvious solution, so simple we didn't feel need to mention it!"

Light VI: Miracle Whip

We left off with OutaNowhere in a bind. No matter how you looked at it, they provided only seven miracles. In one scenario, the last day had no miracle. In the other, the first day was missing. Finally, the CEO himself suggested the solution was obvious.

Yosef Karo helped him out, in an understanding voice. "You're going to tell us you are willing to let Hidden Surprises Inc. take credit for the miracle of the first day of Chanukah, right? You want the Heavenly Court, as well as the Court of the Maccabees below, to recognize that the discovery of a jug of oil sealed with the seal of the High Priest and obviously untouched was also a miracle, and one to be celebrated."

The CEO was charmed to have found a friend. "Of course, they could also count their miraculous victory over the Greek army," he added. "We'll be glad to share credit with Underdog Miracle Services, as well."

"Hold it!" A furious Angel of Bureaucracy was asserting himself. "Who in heaven's name is Underdog Miracle Services?"

"Why, they're the team that engineered the miraculous victory over the Greek-Syrian army."

"Just a minute. We're talking miracles here. Big time miracles. Oil miraculously appearing out of nowhere. Coffee mugs that never empty. Total disregard for the standard conventions of the natural order. And you want to compare that to a natural event of one army winning over another in war!?"

"A very miraculous war."

"They used guerilla tactics. They knew the territory well. They had higher morale and greater conviction."

The people from Underdog had been sitting in the wings ready for just this situation. Deftly, one of them leaped onto the stage. "How about we take a look at what actually happened," he suggested, "and then determine just how conventional it really was."

Before the judges of the court could nod or shake their heads, the lights dimmed and a 3D image of the Maccabee brothers appeared in the projection area. They didn't look like guerilla freedom fighters at all. In fact, they looked a lot more like sedentary yeshiva bachurim in ancient garb, hunched over their scrolls by an oil lamp, waving their thumbs and arms in a heated discussion of talmudic cases of damages.

> "Now, let's say someone just rolls a rock by a hillside, and the rock rolls and causes some heavy property damage along the way. Maybe like even an avalanche or something…"
>
> "Well, his liability depends on this: Did the rock roll due to his rolling of the rock, or was his roll of the rock only an indirect cause of the rock rolling?"
>
> "I told you last time. A rolling rock is similar to fire, and concerning fire we have a Torah edict…"
>
> "But Rabbi Eliezer says…"
>
> "Why do you always bring up that same Rabbi Eliezer?! I've told you a thousand times his statement is irrelevant to this matter!"
>
> "Please don't yell at me. My ulcer, you know."

As the heavenly court shook their heads in pity and compassion, the agent from Underdog continued his narrative, "Now let's take a look at the enemy forces. You decide who you think will be more successful in battle."

The judges were thrown out of their seats by the wild beat of raunchy Hellenist music, as thousands of fierce warriors danced in wild frenzy about huge bonfires, swinging their swords recklessly, guzzling gallons of beer, hollering and laughing at the top of their lungs.

"Stop!!" the judges screamed. "Who gave you permission to bring those hoodlums up here?!"

The presentation ground to an abrupt halt, and the agent asked the judges for their respected opinion: Rate each side for its ability to win a battle of arms and bloodshed.

The Greeks rated 95. Maccabees, 0.05.

"Now let's observe what actually ensued."

The scene was now the top of a Judean Hill. The Maccabee brothers stood about a large boulder, clumsily holding bows and arrows that may have been bought in a cheap toy store, awaiting the approaching Greek army.

"Look, here's a good example of just the sort of rock we were discussing last night. Just the sort of rock Rabbi Eliezer would have…"

"I told you: Rabbi Eliezer's statement has nothing to do with those sort of damages! How can you compare damage due to fire to…"

"Brothers! The Greeks are coming! The Greeks are coming!"

"It's obvious. This is a case of indirect damage. That's exactly what Rabbi Eliezer is discussing!"

"The whole army! Thousands of them!"

"You're already assuming this is indirect damage! But it's not!"

"Oh yes it is!"

"NO IT ISN'T!!"

"Tens of thousands of footmen! Cavalry! They've sent the largest army in the world against us!"

"Brother! I don't understand how you can ignore the reality of all this! It's just such a classic case of indirect…"

"ELEPHANTS! THEY'VE GOT ELEPHANTS! WHOOOOOEEEEEEY!!!"

"Direct liability! That's what it is!"

"They've almost entirely entered the valley right now."

"INDIRECT!"

"DIRECT!"

"Yes! The entire army is in the valley below us! They'll find us soon!! WE'RE MACCABEE PURÉE!"

"INDIRECT!"

"DIRECT!!!!!!"

With that last assertion, the Maccabee brother pounded his talmudic fist down upon the boulder. As their debate continued, the boulder began its descent down the hill, gathering more and more rocks to join it on its mission. Within moments, a cataclysmic avalanche was in action.

"BUT RABBI ELIEZER......"

The leading flank of the Greek army was crushed in a matter of seconds. The central flank turned to retreat in panic, screaming at those behind to turn back. In the stampede Greek fought Greek—the rear flank pressing forward, certain the enemy was ahead, the mid-flank desperate to get the *%*&#^!! out of there.

"BUT RABBI ELIEZER NEVER HAD ANYTHING TO DO WITH ROCK & ROLL DAMAGES!!"

Within an hour or so, the Greek army was demolished. Those not buried under the rock and soil or killed in battle by their own troops simply ran home in utter confusion and trauma, with no idea how to explain any of this to their king, their people or their wives.

The Maccabees eventually determined the liability issue was more complex than it had originally seemed.

The Underdog reps were all slapping the back of the team angel that had played the boulder in that episode.

And the heavenly court determined that, yes, this indeed was a great miracle.

But Yosef Karo was not finished. He was up from his desk, examining the virtual model of the Temple Menora.

"What's that oil made of?" he asked.

"Why, that's olive oil," the CEO answered.

"From olives?" Karo persisted.

"Olive oil comes from olives, right?"

"I thought you just told us it's miracle oil. So it didn't come from olives, then."

"Well," the CEO looked a bit perplexed, "I'll have one of my engineers explain."

An engineer came up in his OutaNowhere sweatshirt and laivees (as they are known up there), with all the charts needed to explain the technical stuff the team thought they wouldn't need to explain.

"As you are all well aware," he began, "the physical world is the ultimate in finite creation. This is actually only a crystallization of the finitude which begins in the higher, spiritual realms. What OutaNowhere has discovered, through close observation of the workings of the cosmos, is quite astounding. Apparently, the energy source of this finite creation is 100% infinite. And that infinite force is continually invested within the finite, sustaining its existence and vivifying it."

"We all know," interrupted one of the angelic judges, "that The Boss, Blessed Be He, is infinite in every way. And we know that everything comes from Him. But, how could an infinite energy source power something finite—all the more so, be invested within it? Simple logic dictates that a large thing cannot fit into a smaller one, never mind infinite within finite. The energy within the cosmos must therefore be finite."

"That was our original hypothesis," explained the engineer. "And I'm sure that's what the Sar Shel Yavan still believes, and is one of the reasons he has such difficulty accepting the supernatural. However, the data we collected overwhelmingly points to an infinite energy source within the finite creation."

"Some examples?" asked a wide-eyed angel.

"As the Talmud states clearly, there is no evidence of the forces of the cosmos weakening over time, or of the sum whole of the mass of the universe diminishing. Furthermore, we see infinite wisdom in each finite detail of the creation. When we saw earthlings tapping into this infinitude by means of the mitzvahs, we were convinced. There are many other pointers, but let's get to our implementation."

The engineer shone a narrow light beam on his chart, which looked vaguely similar to those the engineer from Quality had shown. "Here, you'll recall, is the source of olive oil. It produces light, does not mix with other liquids and yet permeates everything—all this due to its close link with the Sphere of Wisdom, as my colleague before noted. Whereas Quality's strategy was to increase the *quality* property of this node, we are able to unleash the power of the infinite that creates the *quantity* factor of this element."

There was no doubt the judges were in awe. Unleashing the Infinite was heavy stuff to throw around up in heaven. OutaNowhere's stocks were rising rapidly. Rabbi Karo, however, was unimpressed.

"You've yet to answer my question. So is it olive oil, or is it Miracle Whip?" he reiterated.

"It's olive oil! It comes straight from the same place that olive oil comes from, just the same way!" The engineer was exasperated. The CEO jumped in to help.

"Look, it tastes like olive oil, feels like olive oil, has all the spiritual and physical properties of olive oil. Because it **is** olive oil!" he pleaded.

Rabbi Karo didn't flinch. "As I understand, in my very simple, mortal-being, non-angelic terms, olive oil is that which comes out of an olive. Not oil that comes out of a miracle."

The OutaNowhere team members were holding their heads in their wings again. Rabbi Karo continued, "But this oil comes out of nowhere, as your very name suggests."

"But everything comes out of nowhere!" cried the engineer. "You and I and olive oil and everything that exists all come out of absolute nothingness at every moment!"

"True," admitted Karo, "but that's not the end-user experience. The user-experience is induced by a facade of a natural order, by which trees grow, olives develop, and then they are squeezed by live human beings to extract their oil. In my meek understanding, that's the sort of oil the Torah requires be used in the Menora."

The entire assembly-on-high was utterly floored. Finally, one of the judges spoke up.

"We are at a loss," he complained. "We fail to understand what Rabbi Karo is demanding. We're here today to plan a miracle. He seems to be demanding preservation of the natural order. Rabbi Karo, please make up your mind!"

"I also wish to see a very great miracle," Yosef Karo replied, his confidence unshaken. "I'm only requiring that all halachic considerations be fulfilled. Is that too great a miracle for the Heavenly Court?"

The question dropped like lead on the heads of the court.

"No," very softly replied the ChairAngel. "Nothing is too great for heaven. Why, we have the Power of the Infinite. Is that not correct, my fellows?" He looked about both at his colleagues and at the engineering teams. They were forced to nod.

Finally, an erudite-looking angel, positioned not far from center, cleared his throat and spoke. "If it is halachic compliance you demand, Rabbi Karo, then I believe we can settle this matter quite simply with no modifications to the design under review. I had actually imagined these fellows had taken this into consideration when I noted the refill action...excuse me," he gestured to the HI expert from OutaNowhere, "could you play that second animation sequence again. Stop just before the oil refills."

The OutaNowhere engineers eagerly fast-forwarded the animation to the frame where the oil was down to the last drop.

"Yes, stop there!" the erudite judge motioned. "Now, move ahead frame by frame...yes, so you see, there are a few drops left when the new oil appears! It is not appearing out of nowhere. It is simply an extension of the oil that was there from before."

"And just what difference does that make?" his neighbor turned to him impatiently.

"A world of a difference!" he replied. "You see, there is a general principle applied in various circumstances throughout the Talmud that..."

"An outgrowth is classified with its source!" piped in an excited younger angel, proud to display his Talmudic knowledge.

"And liquid which comes into another liquid acquires the same considerations as the original liquid!" joined in another.

The angels were getting excited again. Talmud is a hot topic up there. They have always been jealous that such abstract matters were officially the domain of coarse earthly beings. Once again, debate and discussion exploded in all directions.

"So, what's with the name, 'OutaNowhere'?" demanded one angel above the commotion. "If it's out of nowhere, it's not olive. If it's only an outgrowth of the original olive, then we've got you for misrepresentation."

All eyes were once again on the OutaNowhere team. The CEO was already on his cellular, talking with his lawyers. The sales rep leaped forward. "Actually, we were going to take the name, 'Miracles Unlimited', but it was already a well known trademark, and since the user experience—"

In a bolt, before he could put his foot in his mouth, the CEO had his sales rep off the floor. "Gentleman," he announced, "it's all settled. It will take a few days for the paper work, but our company name is now officially *Miracles Unlimited*. Now if we could just get around to the terms of the contract, I have my attorney on the phone…"

"I'm sorry to say, esteemed judges, but this is not what I expected." It was the voice of Yosef Karo, once again, and all were stilled as it echoed through the hall.

"I cannot hide that I am deeply disappointed. Here, my fellow Jews, the Maccabees went far beyond the letter of the law to challenge the mighty Greek army. I might add, if they had asked a competent halachic authority whether they were obligated, nay, *permitted* to put their lives and those of all the Jewish people in definite danger on the highly improbable chance they might win, the answer would have been a resounding 'No!'."

"Furthermore, they refused to compromise with the apparent reality to light the Menora with impure oil, although, as stated earlier, this would have been perfectly permissible considering the circumstances. They searched every nook and cranny for pure oil, and the Almighty showed His appreciation and endearment to them, providing them with such. Everything until now has been a striving for the most immaculate service of G–d which reaches beyond intellect and reason."

He paused. And then with a biting irony in his powerful voice, like a mighty sword piercing metal, "And you are requiring that they rely on a flimsy kvetch and twist of the Talmudic thumb to burn oil on the second day that did not come out of an olive? This you call the Power of the Infinite?! This you call the Kingdom of Heaven!?"

His voice resounded through the Marble Chamber, pounding upon the ears of its court members. The very walls shook, and the most exalted of the angels looked for somewhere to hide in shame.

"As for the issue of whether this is to be a miracle or a natural event, did the Maccabees ask that question when they went to battle against skilled men of war riding upon elephants? Did they say, 'Well, if the Almighty wants miracles, let Him perform miracles without us, and if He wants us to fight, then what are these elephants doing here?' No! They knew a G–d to whom miracle and nature are one, a G–d who wishes His world to know that physics, too, is miraculous!"

"You engineers!" the rabbi pointed sharply towards the sweatshirts and laivees in the OutaNowhere-now-known-as-Miracles-Unlimited-team. "Didn't your eyes open to this when you discovered that the world He made is an impossibility, a marriage of the finite and the infinite? Then why is it so absurd to require that power here?"

"If He wanted only an open miracle with no trace of physics, then why did He require the Maccabees to search for a flask of oil? Let it simply fall from the heavens! And if He wanted just vanilla physics, without any miracle, then let them find eight days worth of oil!"

"But no, He, in His masterful scheme of things desires both. He desires harmony of the natural and the supernatural. He desires that the lighting of the Menora be performed by natural means, with natural olive oil—from olives, and yet be a miracle by burning for eight days. That is not my requirement, that is His. And you as His agents are charged with fulfilling it."

The ChairAngel struggled to speak the words out of his throat. "I believe we have one more bidder to hear out. Apparently, they plan to use only the pure, natural olive oil with no miraculous additives. They also purport to keep the cups of the Menora full for all eight days. I move we hear them out."

The motion was passed and 'Flaming Wonders' began their presentation.

Light VII: The Battle

Official Report Card: OutaNowhere Proposal

Pros:

- Strong precedent.

- Consideration of human factors.

- New miracle on each day.

- Superb coffee.

Cons:

- Lack of coordination between team members.

- First day of Chanukah provides no oil miracle. Forced to rely on lower-level miracles for that day.

- One major halachic concern: The oil in the Menora is required to be oil squeezed from an olive. This proposal provides a substance that has all the qualities of such oil, but is actually produced overtly ex-nihilo.

Rating: 4 wings

Flaming Wonders knew they had two tough acts to follow. But they figured their presentation had it made.

A flurry of high-distortion, heavy-metal sound, a blinding flash of light and the whole of heaven was on fire. Hollywood-style flames were dancing out of the coffee mugs of every member of the court. With a mighty whoosh, one giant flame appeared at center-floor. A sales rep stepped out. Elegantly, he stepped over to a solid gold Menora (real, physical gold), squeezed oil from olives into the cups (natural, earth-grown olives), and with a flourish of his wings set flames dancing across the cups.

And then, in the 3D-projection area, appeared an image for which all the angels rose in reverence and awe. It was the image of none other than Moses himself, staring at one of the Flaming Wonders flames dancing within a bush. In utter awe, he could be heard whispering to himself, "I must turn from my present, humanist mind-set to attain cognizance of this new observation, that this bush is aflame yet there is no combustion of its carbon!"

As the ear-ringing music reached its apex, all the flames in the chamber rushed together over the heads of the audience and in magnificently choreographed motion converged into the "Flaming Wonders" logo, with a subtitle, "Do We Have Your Attention Now?"

The entire heavenly court applauded, ecstatic to see that, yes, there was a solution, and one that could satisfy even their hyper-rigorous human consultant. Or so it seemed.

The sales rep, remained there, smiling. "Need I say more? I believe you have seen with your eyes, we have filled all the requirements."

"No," sighed an exasperated Yosef Karo. "You need say no more. You have already said it. Or at least, we have all heard Moses himself say it."

"And what better authority on Torah-compliance than that?" ventured the sales rep.

"Quite correct," added Yosef Karo. "And since he clearly acknowledged that you fail to fill a basic requirement, I suppose you can take your little presentation and go back to your desk."

"But, Rabbi Karo!" pleaded a stunned senior judge. "You insisted that the oil not be consumed, and these angels are providing just that. What could now be lacking?"

"Moses said clearly that the bush was not burning," answered Rabbi Karo. "No combustion of its carbon."

"And that's just what you wanted," countered the sales rep.

"So if the bush is not burning, then where is the flame coming from?!" demanded the Rabbi.

"It's just there!" the sales rep exclaimed, obviously having lost his cool already. "What do you care where it's coming from?! Do we really need a whole new technical discussion with the charts and schematics and more talk about infinite light and spiritual engineering? It works. It has worked in the past. It fulfills everything you've talked about until now! It even provides a constant miracle at every moment! So just go with it!"

Yosef Karo took a deep breath and replied, "The Torah states, '...pure olive oil, crushed in order to be a luminance, to raise up an everlasting flame'. That irrevocably implies that the flame must be produced by the combustion of the oil." Now his voice rose again. "But, in your case, as Moses clearly stated, there is no combustion at all!"

"But that's what you asked for!" exclaimed a row of angels in unison.

"I asked for halachic compliance, and I have not budged!" was the firm reply.

Now the whole court was in an uproar. Consternation and bewilderment were on the faces of many as they waved their wings to each other in frantic discussion. Some, such as the ChairAngel, tried to justify Rabbi Karo's position, but in vain.

"How could you please such a man?" they argued. "First he tells us the cups must be full each day with the very same oil as was originally placed in them. Then he demands that the oil be burning. Burning. I.e. *being consumed*. Mass diminishing as it produces heat and light. So is the oil to burn or is the oil not to burn?! The man has to make up his mind!"

That's when the Sar Shel Yavan saw his chance. Amidst the commotion, he crept surreptitiously forth towards Rabbi Karo. At about two meters, he began his attack.

"This," he stabbed, "is precisely the attitude that has gotten you stubborn Jews into all your trouble until now. Cannot you relent and see? If the stick is too long to hold at both ends, then grasp one end alone!"

His eyes began to shine, the polish of his marble glistening in the sharp light of the Chamber. One moment he was a dramatist, the next a philosopher. "Even I would be ready to accept what you call a miracle. It would take some convincing and explaining, but as long as there is some semblance of internal logic—albeit not the logic of our world, perhaps the logic of a higher realm—I am always open to hear anything that could make sense."

"But you," he pointed accusingly at Yosef Karo, "you Jews will not suffice with common sense!"

He paused. His tone became more civil. "You profess wisdom and rationality. Yes, I have admitted many times that your Torah is full of jewels of insight into human nature, a marvelous system of critical analysis that—although quite distinct—nevertheless complements our own. It is, as stated within, '...your wisdom and your understanding in the eyes of the nations'."

His tone suddenly changed. "We could have blended so beautifully together!" He began to cry. "A Judeo-Hellenist Ethic! Your spiritual wisdom, coupled with our Science of Nature..."

The power of Greek drama in its pristine source now unleashed in all fury. "But no! Like the olive oil we discuss today, you refused to mix! You refused to recognize your Torah for the marvelous pinnacle of human wisdom that it is, clinging to this archaic, primitive doctrine that it is something G–dly, something that defies—as if it were at all possible—the very Laws of Logic that set the parameters of the universe, of nature, of the gods and of all that is."

"When I saw your rituals, I learned many things from their wisdom. But there were those I could not fathom. When I inquired about them, your reply always boiled down to the same irrational, 'Because our G–d, the G–d of Israel has so commanded.'"

"I begged you to describe for me this G–d we could not see, a G–d who commands things beyond the intellect of his subjects. You told me He has no description. No explanation. He just is, you said."

"'That which cannot be described and cannot be explained cannot exist!' I exclaimed. And you persisted. You claimed that existence cannot be explained either—despite all I had taught you of science and philosophy."

"When I saw those things, I felt moved to enlighten you. I had mercy upon you by abolishing those commandments that perpetuated this crude, backward doctrine of yours. But, like little children, you couldn't swallow the medicine the doctor prescribed for your own well being! You forced me to take an extreme position.

I decreed upon you, 'Engrave upon the horns of your oxen that you have no portion in the G–d of Israel!'"

"But that drove you only further. You abandoned logic and good common sense, as though all this Torah of yours had nothing to do with that, as if it were no more than an irrational bond between you and something that cannot exist. You sacrificed your very lives and the lives of your loved ones as though nothing else mattered but this nonsensical, blind vision!"

"So you see, I too sincerely desire that your light should shine forth! Let the oil of your wisdom burn and illuminate the entire world! But first we must ensure that it complies with human reason. At the very least, it must fit neatly within the realm of logic, and not step beyond."

Yosef Karo's eyes widened. The Sar had enlightened him. "So you defiled the oil on purpose," he uttered.

The Sar smiled. Karo went on. "You wanted the Maccabees to light the Menora with impure oil, as a symbol of Torah compromised with human intellect. This would have been your underhanded victory!"

"And tell me," the Sar countered, "not using the oil simply because a soldier may have touched it with a ten foot pole makes sense?"

"Reality does not require the approval of your common sense!"

"THERE YOU GO AGAIN!!"

"Excuse the interruption." A hand waved from amongst the engineers' bench, accompanying the polite Danish accent. "My job is empirical science, especially in the area of quantum physics, and I must say I am forced to agree with the rabbi."

Light VIII: Darkness Shines

The Sar turned with an imposing glare, but the scientist meekly continued.

"We don't use philosophy. We are empiricists. Meaning that we accept the data, whether it fits our current conceptions or not. Once we have the data, we try to make sense of it—not the other way around."

"As a matter of fact," the scientist grinned slightly, "we have observed certain phenomena very basic to the common reality that appear to counter common sense altogether."

"But they are measurable, nonetheless."

"Yes, but with a caveat. You see, as soon as we start measuring anything, the reality is impacted by our act of measurement. After all, just by saying that we are going to measure something, we are already bifurcating the reality. We're saying, 'there's us, and there's the thing we are measuring—and then, of course, there's our act of measurement, which is a third thing."

"So therefore?"

"So nothing can really be known in an absolute sense. That leaves a lot of room for what they call miracles—when you are dealing with unknowable states, well just anything could happen. There's no absolute rule of cause and effect, as you ancient Greeks like to believe."

The Sar now demonstrated his mastery of sophistry, his ability to debate even on another's ground. "But it is measurable nonetheless —perhaps not precisely, but measurable."

"Everything, to be a something, must have some sort of measure to it," the scientist conceded.

"Idiot!" The Sar shouted. "Is then what these Jews believe empirically observable in measurable terms?"

The scientist was unperturbed. "A scientist's job is to measure according to what he is able to perceive with the tools available to him," he observed. "The job of the rabbi is to heighten the consciousness of the observer so that the inner world also becomes perceptible."

"And therefore?" insisted the Sar.

"In a strictly material world it is true there is no perception of ritual impurity or purity in the oil. But up here, in the inner world…"

"But they believe in things that are inherently immeasurable!! Not in their world and not in any world! Because they implicitly deny measurement!"

"Such as?"

"They themselves admit that this G–d of theirs is immeasurable. And they believe in a Beginning! Creation ex nihilo! Now, go ahead, tell me you can measure and observe that the entire cosmos came out of nothing!"

"Nothing is immeasurable."

"Precisely. And now, have him tell you about the Holy Ark they claim to have, that is 2.5 cubits wide but takes up no space whatsoever in the 'Chamber of the Holy of Holies'."

The court members looked at each other with widened eyes. They knew about that chamber, and on occasion certain beings were permitted entry. But they were never allowed to measure. That place was strictly *His* territory.

That chamber was twenty cubits wide. The Holy Ark, measuring 2.5 cubits sat in the middle of it. The measurement from the left wall of the chamber to the left side of the Ark was 10 cubits. The measurement from the right wall of the chamber to the right side of the Ark was also 10 cubits. With the width of the Ark, the distance from one wall to the other should have come to 22.5 cubits. Yet, when measured, it came to only 20 cubits. The Ark took up no space. Yet it measured 2.5 cubits. It took up space and it did not take up space. This, the Sar Shel Yavan could not accept. And the members of the heavenly court were entirely bewildered.

"But you have lost!" retorted Yosef Karo. "The Maccabees did not fall for your ploy! They refused to do the rational and searched instead for the impossible —for an untouched flask of pure oil!"

"One more small defeat in battle," the Sar sighed. "But the war I shall still win. For you have gone too far. You are attacking the very basis of logic, and that battle you cannot win."

"Let me explain something," he continued, "since it is I who is the master of mathematics and logic. In our world, one plus one is two. I am ready to accept that a world could have been created where one plus one could be three, or five, or seventeen, or whatever its Creator wishes it to be. I can even accept a world where two conclusions, or even more could be drawn from one equation, as your friend the quantum physicist here wishes to posit. As I said, as long as there is logic—whatever that logic might be. As long as there are true statements and there are false statements—then there is logic and then there can be a reality."

"But what I cannot accept is that one plus one should equal two and the same one plus one should not equal two. That a statement should be both true and false at once—that is a denial of logic. If that could be so, then you and I and all our world and all that exists have no true substance!"

Now he began to scream again, in a maddened, desperate shrill tone. "And that is precisely what you are demanding! You want that oil should burn, yet not be burning! That the laws of nature be preserved, yet a miracle occur! You are demanding darkness to shine and yet remain darkness! But it cannot be!! You cannot defy the very binary foundation of reality, of being!!"

"Yes," the scientist piped in. "Reality is definitely binary. The whole cosmos is built on 'is' and 'isn't'. If the Rabbi wants us to abrogate that to have his miracle, well, it just can't be done. Not even by Heaven Inc.."

Yosef Karo swung around in royal form to face and command the court. "Esteemed masters of judgment!" he declared. "Empowered to do the work of the Infinite Master of All Being! Could it be that the hand of heaven is limited in any way? Perform the Miracle of Chanukah in utmost perfection as the Torah so demands!"

Silence was all he received in response. Quietness, the echo of his own voice and a room of pale faces. His eyes flashed from one angel to the next, to the next, this one in tears, another's face covered with shame, some shaking their heads in sorrow, wings drooping, the glow of heaven all but gone from their countenance. Finally, the ChairAngel spoke up.

"Illustrious Rabbi." He forced out his words, as though reading from a script, a glistening tear rolling over his cheek. "We thank you very much for coming today, and enlightening us with your unique perspective. It is with deep regret, however, that we inform you we are unable to process your request. We refer to the advice we have received that for a flame to both burn and not burn, for the same oil to be consumed and not be consumed, to preserve the laws of nature and defy those very same laws at once, abrogates the very basis of reality. We in heaven can make anything be. Or we can make it not be. But nothing can both be and not be at once. However, we assure you we will do our best to hire the applicant who comes closest to fulfilling the requirements you have laid out before us."

For a moment, Karo was still. He bit his lip, perhaps he shivered—it would be hard to tell. Then he turned ever so deliberately towards the center of the assembly and stepped in awe and trembling towards that point in the epicenter that transcended place, time and consciousness. The Divine Spirit of the Infinite Light And Beyond overcame and enveloped him, as he raised his hands and cried out in a piercing, mighty voice, like the massive waves of a storm crashing upon the shore, "You Who dwells in darkness as You do in light, Who is found in concealment as in revelation! Beyond Being and Not Being, You who unites all things and for Whom all things are one!"

And then, even louder, unbearably, tortuously… "Almighty Father in Heaven, have compassion upon Your children who have given their lives to the slaughter for the sake of Your Great and Awesome Name!"

The echo of his voice pounded the walls of the chamber, shaking them to the ground. The supernal beings of the heavens stood in their places as though stunned. All mouths were closed, all wings held their place in readied stillness.

And then the glory of the Holy One, Blessed be He rose in all worlds. A light that shone with equal intensity in all places, in all realms, for it knows no place or time.

"It is the Ohr haGanuz!" exclaimed the ChairAngel in reverence. "The light of the first day of Creation that was hidden until the Time to Come! We must all descend below to see from whence comes this light!"

So it was that the entire Supreme Court of the Heavens descended into the Holy Chamber of the Temple in Jerusalem—the physical one on this earth—to witness the miracle of the Menora, as the oil burned to produce a flame, but did not burn; combustion occurred, but did not occur; oil was consumed and none was consumed; transforming darkness into light while remaining darkness.

Silence reigned. And the silence was also Light.

"This is my G–d," whispered Yosef Karo. "This is my G–d and I will praise Him."

And all the heavenly court and the whole host of heaven, indeed all of G–d's creation and infinite emanations burst into the song of Hallel, the praise of the Ultimately Infinite.

Including, noted Rabbi Karo, the Sar Shel Yavan.

Darkness shone.

Sources: See Mai Chanukah, Kehos Publication Society, NY, 1994

A Fan Letter

Dear Heaven Exposed:

My friends and I read your radical exposé of the Menora Affair and want you to know how much we all appreciate you revealing the truth about what's really going on up there. I mean, it was really a good thing Rabbi Karo was there consulting on that job, otherwise, we could have had a real second-rate miracle, right? Only Rabbi Karo knew how to make the miracle happen for all eight days without bending any of those Halacha specs. Karo is cool.

So here's our question: Rabbi Karo demanded that the oil should burn and not burn at the same time, right? I mean, I want you to know, we think that's totally radical, only a human being could think of something so way out there. Those angels were really stuck in their cognitive loops. But R' Karo, he was able to jump out of the box and get past that.

Anyway, the problem is like this: When the eighth day is over, what happens with that oil? It's still there, right? So why can't they burn it for another day? And if they could, why did the miracle have to go for eight days instead of just seven—and on the eighth day, they'll just burn the oil that's left and it will burn perfectly naturally? Back to the same problem, right?

We are real confident you've got an answer to this, but in the meantime, we are all, yours truly…

Stumped, stumped and very stumped.

Dear Stumps,

Really encouraging to see you fans out there are on your toes and thinking deep about this stuff. The solution, as far as I can tell, is pretty fundamental:

Once the miracle stops, there's no oil.

You see, the natural state of the oil was to be burning. A miracle suspended the oil in a state of simultaneously not-burning. So, once that miracle departs, we're back to the natural state. In the natural state, the oil burnt out a long time ago. So it's not there.

I'll give you a parallel: At every moment, the Cosmic Creative Force suspends the cosmos in existence. The 'natural' state (we don't really have words for this, so that will have to do) is that the world does not exist. So the world is sort of existing and not existing simultaneously—just like the oil was burning and not burning. Follow so far?

So, what happens if the CCF stops sustaining existence for a moment? No cosmos, right? But that doesn't mean like, "Hey! Where did the cosmos go?!"—that there used to be a cosmos and now it's gone. No siree. Things would fall back to the 'natural' state. *There would never have been a cosmos to begin with.*

So that's how it works here, with the oil, as well: All the time the miracle is at work, the oil is not burning, but it still retains its natural state of burning—simultaneously. Miracle ends, and everything falls back to the natural state—*meaning that the oil has burned.*

Hope I've made that clear enough to answer your question. You've got to try to start thinking counter-intuitively, in paradox form, and you'll get your mind wrapped around it. Of course, since you are deep, skeptical, incisive-thinking exposé fans, you'll undoubtedly come up with more questions. And the answers to those will create more questions. And so on. And that's all just part of the game…

THE SHUSHAN FILES

Miracles vs. Nature

"It always bothers me that it takes a computing machine an infinite number of logical operations to figure out what goes on in no matter how tiny a region of space, and no matter how tiny a region of time. How can all that be going on in that tiny space? Why should it take an infinite amount of logic to figure out what one tiny piece of space/time is going to do?"

—*Richard Feynman, 20th century physicist*

"The Infinite Light descends and penetrates and vivifies all things. It gives all things their existence. This is all they are: projections of the mystery of His Infinitude."

—*Rabbi Moses Cordovero, 16th century Kabalist*

Angel 2343bx8.5 came to me out of desperation after repeated failed attempts to obtain assistance through the medical professionals supported by his employer's benefit plan. As I was of yet unfamiliar with psychiatric treatment of such beings, I initially hesitated to accept an angel as a patient. However, hearing that this particular angel had been unable to find effective therapy through angelic professionals, and having determined that his insurer was in fact prepared to pay at the top of the fee scale, I accepted him as my patient.

This angel's appearance belied signs of hyperactivity and attention deficit. As well, he swung between poles of manic depression within matters of seconds. In general, his presence occupied the entire space and riveted one's attention in such a way that his madness was almost contagious. I, personally, could not handle him for more than twenty minutes at a time.

In our initial session, it was determined that much of this angel's trauma was due to occupational hazards that are apparently common in his profession. Obtaining a coherent history, however, remained elusive. An excerpt from the transcript of that session follows:

Session 1

Therapist: So, already at a young age, you had determined a career for yourself?

Angel: Doc, I can't describe to you how excited I was as a young angel when I saw the big guys doing all that stuff! I so eagerly awaited the day that I too could mess around with the laws of nature, transforming water into blood, making ashes into bugs, splitting oceans, totally overturning the whole scheme of things just to mess up people's minds! This stuff was better than playing with a ton of dynamite!

T: So how did your parents react to all this?

A: Parents?

T: Oh, yes. An angel. No parents. Well, your teachers in school, then. What did they think of these destructive tendencies and ambitions of yours?

A: They put me on track B.

T: Track B. I see.

A: I was so relieved, because so many of my friends had been forced to enter track A or C or...

T: You'll have to fill me in...

A: Track C is really just another branch of track A, just like D and E. Just that they wanted to make guys feel as though it was some specialty...

T: And track A is…

A: *EXACTLY! What's the point? They couldn't get anybody to enter track A anymore, SO THEY MAKE UP THIS TRACK C STUFF!! And when that doesn't work. . .It's all a game! Just say the truth: Track C is just a retrofitted version of track A. But no! Those bureaucrats. . .*

T: You'll have to excuse me, but…

A: *THERE'S NO EXCUSE!! After all, who would want to enter track A, anyways? Is that what we became angels for? Is that the whole point of having supernatural powers and hyper-frequency energies? They might as well have us pushing paper and filling out forms in triplicate! In fact, I bet that's what they. . .*

T: Excuse me, but I'm human and…just what is track A?

A: *That's the Nature Track.*

T: Hiking?

A: *No. Nature. Like Physics.*

T: I'm interested. How do they teach physics up there?

A: *Dull. It's all the skill of understatement, you see. How to make something real spectacular look normal. Eventually, if you're dull enough, they pack you off to The Academy of Natural Science. That's a post-secondary institution where you learn how to make just about anything look normal: Orbiting planets, energy fields,* even birth and death——those guys can take the most amazing, inexplicable miracles and make them look so normal, nobody will even ask a question. Why, **the entire cosmos** is being regenerated out of absolute nothingness at every moment, and **nobody even wonders about it!** Can you imagine?

T: They have a technique?

A: Basically, there are two tricks: One is consistency. You know, you do something just once and everybody's talking about it. You continue doing it over and over like nothing happened, and they take it for granted. It's a cover-up game. I figured that out without even going to their dumb institution.

T: And the other trick?

A: That's a matching game. Gets a little more complex, but still pretty insipid. You match up behaviors with the features of objects, so that things appear to be behaving according to their own makeup. Water looks and feels like it should flow, so you do that with it and just keep doing it. Stuff that looks weightier gets more weight. Ethereal stuff gets less weight. Eventually, people may even start believing that everything just follows a simple one-dimensional paradigm of cause and effect. Isn't that crazy? It's a twenty-six dimensional universe with 613^{86} channels of resolution and these guys make it look like time has only one dimension!

T: Sounds like that takes a lot of skill, ingenuity, knowledge…

A: And no inspiration. You know who that track is for? It's for the guy who can make Chopin and Liszt sound like computer-generated trivia. Guys who can take a masterpiece of a landscape and make a six color paint-by-numbers set out of it. Guys who can transform the world's most hilarious joke into a bedtime story.

Like Joe Angel. You know, the kid with the bow tie and neatly combed hair? Why I remember when Joe bought his first fireworks set. He handed out earplugs to the whole neighborhood and made sure to set it off in the middle of the day when nobody was home. At carefully planned, three minute intervals——just to be consistent. Then he mailed out letters of apology. . .

T: And you disagree with this sort of procedure.

A: BLOW THE NEIGHBORHOOD TO PIECES, THAT'S WHAT I SAY! If you're not going to shock anyone, so what's the point? That's why they put me in track B.

T: That's the destructive track? Like the Angels of Doom type of thing?

A: Destructive? Doom? Are you kidding?! Track B angels are the ultimate angels! Why, if it weren't for us, humanity would never have survived this long. You would all have been zapped——by totally natural causes, of course——at the very first act of inconsistency.

T: By the track A guys?

A: And track C. And track D. Why, if it were up to them, anything that didn't fit in to a neat, orderly scheme of things wouldn't exist longer than a nanosecond. They're all procedural programmers——everything's got to be real predictable, including the end user. And, as we all know, nothing's messier than a human being. Bad end users. Bad, bad, bad.

T: And just why are you seeing me then?

A: You guys are just so chaotic, wild, unpredictable, mischievous, erratic and totally lovable! Just nothing you do fits into any pattern. There's nothing in the universe as unpredictable and messy as a human being. That's why I find you guys so fascinating. And so do all the other track B guys. We strongly identify with you. That's why we're always out there saving your skin at the last moment.

T: Track B is…Cognitive Therapy. Object Programming? Chaos Theory? Anarchist Politics?

A: Track B is the Supernatural Track. Miracles. Signs, Wonders. Blow consistency and nature out the door! Without us, you guys would be nowhere! Take yourself, for example. You know how many times over the last twenty four hours one of my friends had to whisk you out of the hands of those nature fiends with an open miracle?

T: I didn't notice.

A: YES!! Now you're getting it! YOU DIDN'T NOTICE! NOBODY EVER NOTICES! That's the whole problem! That's what we've been having to deal with all this time! And it's driving us nuts. It's those Nature Fiends, and, Doc, THERE'S NOTHING WE CAN DO ABOUT THEM!!

At this point, Angel began raving and ranting unintelligibly until he bordered on dissolution into the ether. I quickly called our session to an end, allowing myself enough time for research (and recuperation) before the next visit.

Session 11

Throughout the week following that visit. I carefully noted incidents in my life that appeared out of the normal pattern. As it turned out, I found myself unable to determine any pattern of normalcy to judge by. Almost nothing was predictable. But, most puzzling, in hindsight, all seemed quite natural. This in itself, opened my mind to hear in greater depth what the angel had to say.

The angel arrived for the next session late and with obvious signs of anxiety & stress. His wings, which he held in hyperextension, were visibly more wilted. The ethereal glow around his face was a sickly green. I felt it necessary to direct our conversation towards matters which he found stimulating and uplifting. A significant portion of that session follows:

T: We've talked enough about that, now. I'd like to hear a little about your own track, track B.

A: Track B was everything I ever wanted to learn. Basically, it was about how to sabotage the track A guys.

T: Espionage?

A: That's it! But very hi-tech. ☺ o o o o h h ! I like it! What was that word you used again? E S P I O N A G E. Yes! We totally messed up everything those guys had so neatly programmed. Doc, it was so neat!

T: Uh, I'm a little worried for the couch you're jumping on. Perhaps you'd like to walk around a little as you talk?

A: ?

T: Alright, then maybe just hover.

A: Let me tell you how it works. The material world is just a product of layers upon layers upon layers of programming and interface, all of which serve to protect the end user from the deep abstractions of higher-level coding. I mean, if you would try to generate this world straight out of the embedded instruction set, there's no way you could get a physical world out of that. Not even from system native code, or even assembly or even a 2GL language. You need to totally get away from the native stuff into highly metaphorical and deeply defined interfaces. . .

T: Uh, I'm a psychologist…

A: It's okay. You'll recover. The point is that's not the point. It's that, nevertheless, whatever happens down where you are starts off in much more abstract terms at a deeper level of existence. <u>So by</u> **<u>a little messing around with the wiring up there, we can have a major impact on what happens down here!</u>**

T: How does that differ from standard physics?

A: It doesn't, really. And that's the beauty of it. We can blow their whole front and keep the system intact at the same time!

T: Blow their…

A: Remember? The consistency game! And the matching game! When we start fiddling around with their code, consistency is out the window! And behaviors no longer match object properties!

So everybody points and says, "Look! A miracle, a miracle!" Even though everything beforehand was also a miracle. But now they notice it. It totally blows their minds.

T: Whose minds?

A: Listen, Doc, I'm really not supposed to let any of you material beings in on this, but since I trust your professional confidentiality, and you are my doctor and all, well, this is our plan: We figure that with enough strategically placed miracles of this sort, eventually the whole cover-up will be shattered! I mean, eventually people will start questioning **everything**. They'll see through the whole façade and realize THAT THE WHOLE THING IS ONE BLASTED MIRACLE!!

We almost accomplished that, you know, back in the good old times. I was just a little guy then, but I got to watch it on the news. They totally blew away the minds of the greatest scientists of their day! And these were humans that knew stuff! They could handle the stick-to-snake, water-to-blood, and even multiple terrestrial amphibian stuff. But when our guys started getting into ashes turning into insects and light becoming thick dark and stuff like that——they were lost, just lost. Eventually, even the most committed naturalists had to concede the track A guys are not in charge.

Because they're **N⊕T!!** They never were! It's a bloody chutzpah of theirs, parading themselves before the whole world like they're the ultimate masters of the universe!!

Look, doctor, you're a good doctor, but if you would hear some interns whispering that you held complete mastery over your patients, wouldn't you protest? Isn't that the ethical thing to do? Of course it is. But these track A guys——ethics? The whole world was putting up temples to worship them, offering them sacrifices, singing and dancing their praises just to get on their good side, and do you think they said a word?! If you don't mind me saying so, I think they got a big kick out of it!

That's where we came in——with official orders from the Boss, of course——the Big Boss——and we blew their ploy. Boy, by the time we were finished, that whole country, even their top honcho knew who is really in charge!

I waited for the patient to descend from the ceiling, then continued.

T: It appears this was a major turning point in your life.

A: Yes. Look, Doc. I'm trying to calm down, but. . .

T: But by the time you got out of school, things weren't the same anymore.

A: You've been at this profession a long time, Doc. I can tell. You're two steps ahead of me. No, it wasn't the same. The whole paradigm had shifted. No more Pharaohs, no more Egypts, no more wild and radical spirits like Moses and Joshua around either. Sure, the track A cult had suffered some major credibility defeats, but at the same time, our guys had been so shackled with bureaucracy. . .

T: Did you receive a position upon graduation?

A: I jumped straight into senior office.

T: And what was your first assignment?

A: It was, it was. . .Doc. . .I don't know if I can handle talking about this. . .do we have to?

T: Well, if you want me to help, we're going to have to come head on with it at some point.

A: Okay. I understand.

T: Was it still in the ancient world?

A: Doc, I don't know. I mean, I don't know if I can talk about it. It was very traumatic.

T: Whereabouts?

A: Persian Kingdom. Asinine King. Clandestine Jewish Queen. Megalomaniac advisor.

T: Shushan?[8]

A: DOC! NO!!! PLEASE! I CANT I CANT!!!

T: Oh well. It was a good couch.

A: SHUUUUUUUUUUUUUUU SHAAAAAAAAAAANNNNNN NNNNNNNNNNN☺☺☺☺☺☺☺☺☺☺ ☺☺☺☺!!!!!!!!

Obviously, at this point it was necessary to cut the appointment short, once again.

Session III

Over the next week, the image of Angel vaporizing my couch and the sound of his high-pitched scream haunted me incessantly. So did his perspective of the true workings of everyday physics. More and more, I noticed in my daily life strange coincidences and eerie, unexpected events. By the end of the week I was looking under the bed, behind walls and up on the ceilings for hidden angels. At times, I regretted taking this patient on, as I felt the strain on my own mental health.

By telephone, it was agreed that our subsequent meeting would take place in a sealed and padded chamber. I instructed Angel on relaxing breathing techniques, and suggested he take frequent outdoor excursions and get plenty of exercise to reduce stress and anxiety. Pharmaceuticals were not applicable in this case. Except for myself.

I was pleasantly surprised when Angel appeared on the dot for the appointment, a calm, relaxed aura about him. During our session, he found himself capable of relating incidents lucidly and even with some objectivity. At least initially.

The following transcript has been edited for the sake of the professional reputation of those involved:

T: Now take a deep breath, and while breathing it out, say, "Shuuuuuushaaaaaaan." Come on.

A: Shu-u-u-u-usha-a-an.

[This exercise was repeated several times, until the desired state was achieved.]

T: That's it. Now, let's start from your initial briefing on the Shushan affair. And remember, if anything seems to be too traumatic to discuss, just repeat this exercise and continue.

A: Shuuuuuushaaaaaan.

I remember the briefing room well. I sat there with my buddies from our office, guys I really respected and could work together with as a team. And there were these other guys there.

T: Any that you recognized?

A: Yeah. One of them was Joe Angel. That's how I figured out they must have been from the 'A' Team. But, for the life of me, I couldn't figure out what in heaven's name the 'A' Team was doing there. This was a miracle job, for earth's sake!

T: But the project coordinator explained.

A: He said, well, to tell you the truth, I didn't really follow what he was talking about.

T: Try to remember. Perhaps you did follow, but you don't want to remember.

A: He said this project was going to be something completely new and revolutionary. A major step forward in the development of cosmos technology. Which I don't get. I mean, if you want to go forward, what are those 'A' guys doing here? This just sounds like more of their stinking bureaucracy, that's what it is! If they would only let us have some free rein. . .

T: Say with me, "Shuuuuu…."

A: . . .Shaaaaaaaaaaaaannnnnnnnnnnnn.

T: Let's talk in objective terms. Just describe what happened, we'll keep the judgments for later.

A: Alright then. Of course, he described the situation down there. You guys were in hot trouble once again, and we had to jump in and save you. Typical case, except that this was the first time we had to do this on a major scale since the Israelites had left the Land of Israel. But that was no sweat. I mean, Egypt was also outside of Israel, and hey maybe this was our chance to do a number like that again. I got to tell you about what they did in Egypt when I was little. . .

T: Let's stick to…

A: Yeah, okay. The guy asked for suggestions. Of course, our team had great suggestions. And we were fully prepared. We had our charts, portfolios, 3D simulations, all at our fingertips. And there were so many ways to go. Hey, we even had a plan to blow Haman and his entire army off the surface of the planet without causing any harm whatsoever to innocent bystanders! Now if that wouldn't be an eye-opener, I don't know what would.

T: Neat.

A: But it was knocked down. The coordinator guy pointed out that this didn't take into account the natural means already at our disposal. Such as the fact that the Queen was Jewish and so on. So I spoke up——'cause it really bothered me to see my buddy's great ideas shot down just like that——and I asked a simple question.

T: Yes?

A: Shuuuuuuuuuuushaaaaaaaaaaaaan SHUUUUUUUUUUUUUUUSHAAAAAAAAAAAAAAAAAAAAAAAAAAAAAAN·N NNNNNNNNNN

T: Are you ready now?

A: Okay, look I should have kept my mouth shut. But they had this planned anyways, I know. So I said, "So if you've got all these natural means at your disposal, what do you need a miracle for?"

T: Good question.

A: Dumb question. The next thing the coordinator did was turn to the 'A' guys and say to them, "So then, how would you fellows deal with this utilizing all the natural means at your disposal? Do we need a miracle after all." Doc, my buddies were ready to h a v e m e e v a p o r a t e d .

In the meantime, these 'A' guys are going on and on about how with the proper political push and pull, a few very predictable assassinations here and there, and a touch of palace intrigue the whole job could be pulled off without any external intervention whatsoever. Who needs miracles, they said. Yes, Doc, they actually said that TO OUR FACES!

T: Shuuuuuuu…

A: shan. You ain't heard nothing yet. You see, the coordinator disagreed with them too!

T: That must have been a relief.

A: A relief!? It was a nightmare!! If we didn't get the job, at least we could just walk away and let those guys make a mess of things. Next time, they'd call us back for sure. But no. This guy had the most nefarious scheme you could imagine up his sleeve: He wanted us to work together!!!

T: Stay objective. Tell me his words.

A: He said, "Guys, I want you to work together on this and come up with the most original miracle ever. One that breaks none of the standards of team 'A', yet fulfills all the requirements set by the Miracles Standards Committee."

T: You have standards?

A: Doc, you're a nice guy. Don't say things like that. Of course we have standards. We're a highly respected professional community. If we didn't have standards, how could we protect our work force, our reputation? Any nerd Joe Angel could come along running some dumb and natural sequence and throw in a miracle once in a while to keep things working. Now, this guy's not union, he's untrained, and he doesn't pay dues. That's why if a miracle is to be performed, it has to be done by licensed track 'B' engineers. And there are basic, minimum requirements. Any miracle performed must:

1. Involve new energy from beyond the standard cosmic system.

2. Be directly under the supervision of the Heavenly Court of Justice.

3. Have its origin in some super-cosmic system that was in existence prior to the completion of the six days of creation.

T: What happened to blowing minds and opening eyes?

A: That's the art of it. You don't standardize art. Standards are just to keep out amateurs and scabs.

T: And the 'A' Team, they have standards, too?

A: They have substandards. He-he-he. Why, that's it, Doc! That's their whole problem! They have so many rules and regulations and red tape——but it's all on purpose! The whole thing is a cover-up! The Laws of Nature are a conspiracy!

T: But as far as conflict with your standards....

A: Did you get that, Doc? THE LAWS OF NATURE ARE A CONSPIRACY!! That sums it up in one sentence! AND HE WANTED US TO GO INTO CAHOOTS WITH THEM! He was demanding unethical COLLUSION!

I was getting nervous. We had only just started the session.

T: Let's speak objectively again. Let's think into just where it is that your team and the track A angels are in conflict. That way…

A: We have ethics. Can you call what they do ethical? Aside from the collusion bit. Look, I know that's shocking. It's outrageous. It's also the fact. The Laws of Nature have no ethical considerations. They are programmed strictly according to just the highly rationed energy allotted to the cosmos for each specific moment.

T: But this way, there is no conflict of job description.

A: That's how it's supposed to be. But this guy, this coordinator guy, he comes along and tells us we have to break all the rules! We have to make miracles under THEIR supervision. Natural Miracles he wanted! They wanted energy levels that had never before been allowed into the cosmos to enter quietly and fit into natural schemes! They wanted miracles that take into account all the natural phenomena but won't disturb any of them! They wanted physics to act ethically! They had us make focus groups and team confidence building sessions, white galaxy river rafting together. We had to discuss our differences and commonalities and go to parties together. IT WAS SICK! SICK! SICK!!

SHUUUUUUUUUUUUUUUUUUUUUS
HAAAAAAAAAAAAAAAAAAAAAA
AAAAA!!!!!!

T: Stay objective now. Let's talk about your success. After all…

A: SHAAAAAAAAAAAAAAAN
NNNNNNNNNNNNNN
. . . .

T: No! Not the padding! We need the pa….

[to be continued]

Session IV

In the wake of that disconcerting episode with its gruesome finale, the Angel's absurd accusation rang relentlessly in my mind. "The Laws of Nature are a conspiracy!" Like the inane melody of a country hit played and replayed mercilessly through the speakers of the clinic's waiting room, they began to pervade my consciousness. I had heard conspiracy theories to explain behavioral psychologists, Internet advertising, continental drift and adolescent acne—but the Laws of Nature? As far as I was concerned, it was the laws of nature that paid my bills, ensured the earth would be under my feet every morning and guaranteed that what we doctors knew one day would not change the next. How could a conspiracy be so infallible?

As I have mentioned paying my bills, I should note that collecting payment from the patient's insurer proved somewhat awkward. For one thing, the address supplied simply did not exist in this universe. Fortunately, I was able to ignore this matter, as I had coincidentally received a promotion to department manager at the clinic and come into some extra cash by winning a lottery that very same week.

As for the patient, we had obviously not been able to arrange a subsequent appointment, so I did not know whether I would see him again or not. However, it became clear that I was unequipped to deal with Angel 2343bx8.5 without further research. But, search as I may, there were simply no catalogued studies on angels nor on "anathema to natural law."

The solution arrived in the propitious form of yet another heavenly patient, Angel 0112358-13-21… (a.k.a. "Angelo Fibonacci").

His appointment had been set two weeks earlier at 9:30 AM. At 9:25 precisely, he plodded into reception. Bent over deeply, his wings wilted and gray, his presence literally sucked the color out of the waiting lounge. Even the color TV and the National Geographic pictures went black and white. When he finally looked up, I saw it: The bow tie gave him away. Right off, I knew this was someone Angel 2343bx8.5 did not party with.

Angelo Fibonacci dragged himself into my office, his nose tracing along the carpet.

T: "Mr. Fibonacci, you are here to discuss your feelings of inferiority, low self-esteem and general worthlessness. How long have you been harboring these feelings?"

A long silence. I waited. Then...very softly...

AF: Since Shushan.

T: Ohhhhyesss!!

AF: You know about Shushan?

I needed to stay professional. But the excitement was hard to hold down.

T: Just continue with the history. What happened on the Shushan project that aroused such emotions?

AF: It wasn't so much the project. The project was very...well...redeeming. It was...one of the miracle angels. His comments to me were so...hurtful...

Angelo looked up for a moment. His eyes caught something on the wall. For a moment, I thought he was introspecting. I was wrong.

AF: Doc, that bothers me.

T: Tell me about what bothers you.

AF: The picture.

T: The whole picture?

AF: Just the one on the wall.

T: You don't like Ansel Adams?

AF: It's off.

T: Off?

I watched as the picture adjusted itself slightly on the wall.

AF: That's much better. Where were we?

T: Shushan.

AF: oy. Can we go somewhere else?

T: You seem to associate Shushan with pain.

AF: Your desk.

T: I like my desk the way...

It was too late. My familiar wading pool of papers had already filed themselves neatly into a warehouse foreman's dream of neat, even stacks. even the children in my dear family portrait were now all groomed and standing in well-spaced order by height.

T: How long have you had this compulsion for neatness?

AF: No, Doc, please!! I can't take any more of that criticism. It's very hurtful. Why do you think I've come to you? Do you think I was always a depressed angel? No! I used to be very well adjusted. I liked my life. I liked my job. I felt needed. Important. Until I had to work with *him* and he wouldn't let me alone. That's why I came here. And now, you, too...

He was crying. I've had patients cry in my office before. It's part of the therapy. For me, it's just another procedure. But these tears I couldn't take.

AF: There's nowhere I can go! It's true! It's just as he told me. I said, maybe I've got an inferiority complex. He said, no, you just *are* inferior, ask any psychologist. And he gave me your number. And I come here and

it's true! You agree! I am just inferior and
that's it!

Out my window it was pouring rain. I wondered if there was any connection. I also wondered what was going to happen to my golf appointment. I knew I had to think fast.

T: Angelo, that's not true. I haven't provided you with any diagnosis whatsoever. I'm not here to provide diagnosis. I'm here to help. To bring some *sunshine* into your life. Now let's get to some of those *clear, sunny* thoughts and wipe those clouds away.

AF: You think my obsession with neatness and consistency is an illness. You don't appreciate just what goes into keeping an entire natural order natural and orderly.

T: I certainly understand it takes a clear, open mind.

AF: Clarity! **Gevald!!!**

I was failing. Miserably. There was a full-blown thunderstorm happening outside.

AF: It's downright miraculous, that's what it is.

T: Miraculous…but I thought you were…

AF: ohno ohno ohno…what am I doing here? How's this humanoid going to help me? Doc, you don't know the first thing about natural law and order, do you?

T: I'm certainly eager to be *enlightened*. That's part of my job. So if you care to…

AF: Miracles as you know them— those are just reckless hacking. We create a magnificently elegant finite loop and they go punch a leak somewhere and pour in infinite light from beyond. From outside the system. What's the big deal? They didn't create anything. All their fame and glory rests solely on wrecking what others have accomplished. If The Boss wanted infinite light, He didn't have to make a world. That's what He started with— Infinite Light. A world is supposed to be finite.

That's what they did in Egypt. That's all they had to do at the Red Sea fiasco— they keep boasting about that year after year. Once they even brought down the entire system— we had to throw the entire heavenly body scheme into pause— just because they couldn't bother looking for a more elegant way to finish off a regular battle event.

T: *What* went into pause?

AF: The sun, the moon, the stars…

T: The *sun*?

AF: Joshua could have easily won the battle by natural means…but no…they wouldn't listen…

T: So what would have been better about…

AF: Natural means is awesome. It's a science. It's an art. It's the ultimate art. The Boss made it that way and He likes it that way. He even said, after He created it, "It's *very* good." Not just good— *very* good. You don't go wrecking something that's very good and beautiful for no good reason.

T: But miracles are infinite light.

AF: Miracles are **darkness!**

T: no. p l e a s e don't say that.

218

AF: People see a miracle and they have no clue what's going on. You can't study miracles. You can't make a science out of them. If there were nothing but open miracles, there would be no education, no universities, no professors, no doctors...

T: Oh, that's no good.

AF: People see a miracle and they say, "Hey what?" Then they just walk away and pretend nothing happened. I've seen it over and over. Okay, so those Children of Israel that left Egypt, they were broken and oppressed, so they could handle it. But their oppressors never got the point. So what did those miracle maniacs do? They drowned them. You know about those kind of scientists— they drown the specimens that don't match the desired results, right?

The ceiling was leaking real bad. I thought I might soon become one of those specimens.

AF: The point is that if you want people to learn, to grow, to really appreciate the wonders of creation and the Creator, you need nature— not miracles. Take Abraham...

T: Is he coming here, too?

AF: Not a bad idea. But only through natural means.

T: How's he...

The Angel was already fudging with the buttons on my video display—the one I use for educating patients while I take coffee breaks.

AF: How many dimensions does this thing display, anyway?

By the time I figured it out what he was talking about, there was already a three-dimensional display projecting into the middle of the room.

T: Uh, two.

AF: Two? How was I supposed to know. Oh well.
    Some glitches in the natural order are
    unavoidable.

    Now, here you have little Abraham as a small
    baby, examining the world about him— the
    stars, the moon, the sun, the clouds, the
    wind...

T: Yes, yes. Grandpa told me the story.

AF: ..the rain. And he saw that things happen
    with a singular order, a design. Nothing is
    haphazard. He saw it is an intelligent
    system— even though it superficially looks
    like inanimate materials. Something like, if
    I meet a human and I see that he does things
    with design and intent, I know he's got a
    mind, right? I mean, it may look like just a
    hunk of blood, flesh and bones with a chunk
    of gray meat up in the attic. Intuitively,
    you would think it's ridiculous that this
    thing could produce intelligence...

T: Please. Let's just focus on the video...

AF: Good idea, listen to Abraham himself:

Abraham was now older in the video. Old enough to be explaining things to a crowd of people gathered about him.

Abraham: So look at this world! Does it really look like a mess of gods fighting with each other? Don't you see the harmony, the oneness, the synergistic gestalt of it all?

The people were stroking their beards and nodding their heads. There was a wet, burnt smell in my office.

AF: Note the cognitive approach. Highly effective. No need to convince with signs and wonders. People come to realize the truth on their own. Miracles, on the other hand, would just plunge them into confusion.

> Abraham: So we see a Single Intelligence involved in all this. The universe is alive with a single soul within it! G–d is *here now*!

More stroking of beards. More enthusiastic nodding. More burnt smell, too. Along with a crackling sound from the video display.

AF: You see, if they would know The Boss from miracles, they wouldn't think of Him as *here now*! They would think the only way He can be *here now* is by busting reality as they know it. They would think, "It's either G–d or a normal world— but you can't have both."

Seeing G–d in nature brings them to an understanding of an immanent, withit G–d. That's what Abraham's ideas are all about.

> Abraham: But that is not all there is to this Single Intelligence. Look deeper and you will see the Infinite within!

It stopped there. The water level on the floor finally zapped the electronics and the Abraham video along with it.

T: There's really no end to this...

AF: Yes! You caught that. Abraham also discovered there's no end to the depth of this wonder. After all, you are probably asking yourself: If Abraham discovered The Boss through nature, how did he know about the Infinite? You probably think we nature angels have something against infinity, right?

The truth is, we are constantly working with infinity. Just that we have a more mature approach. To *them* it's a game. To *us*, it's an art and a science.

T: [looking up] Maybe you could just think of a way of holding back what's coming down from up there?

AF: Yes, Doc! Now you're on the ball! That's exactly what we do! From up there, infinite light is pouring down. Our job is to contain the infinite within a finite order.

Like, imagine that up there in those clouds was an infinite reservoir of water.

Now it was me crying.

AF: ...and your job was to make sure only a trickle, just enough for a good deluge, managed to reach the earth. Because, otherwise, there wouldn't be any earth, right?

T: No. Just mud. Sopping, unplayable mud.

AF: So that's the situation we have to deal with. Doc, did you ever notice that the laws of nature are really infinite?

T: Um, can't say I did.

AF: Well, you're a human, so it's not really your fault. But if you would think about it, there's really no reason that any of the laws have to be the way they are. Take Newton's laws of motion. Or Planck's constant. With modification, of course— Newton and Planck, they're only humans. Gravity, electromagnetism, the nuclear forces. The point is, there's no reason they have to be the way they are. There's no reason The Boss couldn't have done things entirely different.

T: I've noticed.

AF: That means the source of all these laws and rules is unlimited. And they are, too, in a way. You probably haven't realized this, but do you think things were always this way? I mean, since the Beginning?

T: No. Only since you guys started coming here.

AF: Well, they have been. Since the end of the sixth day of Creation, those constants and laws haven't changed. Not one iota. The size of the universe may change. Relative time wobbles around. Light speed is slowing down. Certain higher dimensions have become a little more flat. Chicken soup isn't as effective anymore. But the basic laws and equations that were arbitrarily decided at the very Beginning— none of that has changed even to the smallest quantum. Now how is it possible that these things don't wear out?

T: They're supposed to wear out?

That was a mistake. A bolt of lightning and immediate thunder shook the building. The lights were out. Everywhere. Everywhere except for a mysterious light in my office.

AF: **WHY SHOULDN'T THEY?** Do you humans take *everything* for granted? Everything else wears out— because everything is finite. Same with the laws of nature. It all gets sustained from somewhere. So if that source were finite, the laws of nature would be wearing out, get it? So we nature angels, we skillfully manage the channeling of infinite

possibilities and infinite energy into
tightly defined and limited packages of
natural causes.

Okay, let's make it simpler: Conservation of
matter, energy and consciousness— you know
that one? Nothing gets lost. Nothing. Isn't
that amazing?

Now that's what I call beauty and elegance! A
nexus of the finite and the infinite!
Absolutely wondrous! Not like what those
ruffian gangster miracle snobs are trying to
push on us— to them it's either/or: Either a
finite world or infinite light.

Get it?

T: Uh. I'm just a human. Kind of inferior, you know. I...I just
wanted to play golf real bad this afternoon. I really wanted to
have an office with an upholstered sofa and lighting and a...a
dry carpet...

AF: Oy, Doc. Look what I've done! I should have
known it was contagious! Next thing, you're
going to start talking in mono-spaced type.

T: It's not like I'm a golf fanatic or anything. But all this angel
therapy has been driving me nuts. I need a break. If I don't get
out there to the match this afternoon, I don't know what's
going to happen to me. Look, I don't know why I ever
accepted these angel patients. I really can't take it. It makes me
feel stupid, incompetent, confused and downright inferior.

AF: You don't need to feel that way, Doc.

T: I'm not inferior?

AF: Being inferior doesn't make you incompetent.
Look, I came in here pretty gray and now,

well, I'm feeling a lot better about myself, my occupation, my position in the cosmic order…talking things out over here to a non-judgmental human has really helped. You've really brought some…some…

T: Yes, some…

AF: …some *sunshine* into my life.

T: aaaahhhhhhhh.

One look outside and I almost jumped out the window. Blue. Big Blue Sky. Birds singing. I spun around quickly and asked:

T: So do you think there's a chance I could even *win* that game this afternoon?

AF: Win? I thought you just needed some stress release? We don't do *winning*. If you're good, you win. Given your condition…well. Natural law, y'know, like we were talking. You don't want those miracle hackers mixing into your life, oh no.

T: Oh no. Just that maybe you could make it happen, well, naturally.

The Angel's brow furrowed. He looked at me suspiciously.

AF: Now where did you get this idea of natural miracles from?

T: Well, I got this promotion, for one thing. Not quite the natural thing for a…well, you know my…professionalism issues…

AF: It was a miracle.

T: But it was very natural. And all sorts of other things lately…

Angel shook his head, muttering in muffled tones.

AF: Oh no. Oh no. Wait! Where's your phone?

T: Angels need phones?

AF: Natural means whenever possible, remember?

The Angel had already grabbed a phone from my desk. He didn't dial nine. I don't think he dialed anything, really. In fact, the phone was just a toy one of my kids had left there. But he was talking to someone, somewhere. Another one of those glitches in natural law, I guess.

AF: Pi? Yeah, this is Fibo. No, I have to talk this way. I'm on a mission. Okay, it's a medical leave. But I need you to look up some coordinates. It's at $Tof42_61°$ in only 3D at active space. Yeah, way down here. He's a shrink. Not too good. You see any possibilities for promotion there in the last few creation cycles? Nothing? But it happened, right?

It's okay, that's what we thought. Look, one more thing: Any signs of hacking? Leaks? System piercing? Nothing. Look, it's okay, I can handle it. Really. I'm feeling much better. We'll talk when I get back.

click

Angelo Fibonacci was back down on his chair, nose back to the ground, wings wilting once again. I could barely hear him mumbling.

AF: He doesn't even ask us. We can't do it. We don't get it.

T: Uh, this is a different matter now?

AF: No. The same one. We're incompetent.

I glanced out the window in trepidation. My worst fears were confirmed. The big, black clouds were on the horizon, swiftly returning. I had to think fast.

AF: We do nature. They do miracles. Somehow, for some reason, He wants both. At once. But He's the only one who can do that. So He just bypasses us. We become superfluous. Redundant. He does it all Himself.

T: You mean, like my miraculous promotion.

AF: It's impossible. He breaks none of the Laws of Nature, and at the same time, He breaks all of them. It all remains finite and at the same time, He reserves infinite possibilities— He gets whatever He wants. Nobody can figure it out. He wanted us to do just a small mockup of that in…in…that place…

I knew better than to fill in the name. I was wracking my brains. I knew that this was it. Either I was a therapist, or I was going the way of Pharaoh's army. I put everything I had into it. I don't know where the words came from—and I knew I was really risking it—but I truly believe those words saved my life.

T: Fibo, look, you explained very nicely all the advantages to neat, consistent patterns of nature. It makes for an understandable reality and brings wonder into focus. It makes the unknowable very knowable. It makes the infinite immanent.

But there was a friend of yours here a few weeks ago that had a very good case for miracles. You have to understand his argument.

He was still listening. He didn't crack up when I said that.

T: Miracles are when the Infinite comes out in the open. Not just the background. Miracles get people to question their whole take on reality. We humans need to be shaken up once in a while. Miracles show there's something beyond, something *transcendent.*

AF: So you think they are better than we are, after all. They're the real angels and we're just nerds, right?

T: I think that each of you has something to offer. Now if you could get it together to do something *real* special...like a miraculous nature or maybe a natural miracle...that could truly be deep and beautiful.

AF: You want immanent and transcendent all at once. Infinite and finite in a single package.

pause

AF: Well, I suppose, to The Boss, they're just two modalities of the same Power of Being.

pause. A few quivers of the feathers at the tips of his wings. For once, I knew better than to open my mouth.

AF: So, you think, if we talk it through, we might be able to create some synergy. Like a miracle that permeates the natural realm. Or a state of nature that is only a veil for the miraculous. Crisp and natural on the outside, miraculous and chewy on the inside.

T: Actually, I was just thinking you might want to start with my golf par.

AF: Perhaps. But that may still be beyond us. We have to leave some things for Him and Him alone. But maybe, in Shushan...

He said that with an astonishing calmness. It was the first time I heard that word without a trace of anxiety or hysteria. In fact, he even smiled. I noticed a twinkle in his eye. And then he was gone.

I checked out of the office with just enough time to make it to my game. The turf was surprisingly dry for such a stormy morning. Bill and Dave played fairly, but my game was downright impressive. I guess all that training and perseverance finally paid off. I guess.

THE ANGEL FILES

All of the Above

Part One: Angel Chat

In the words of a great American philosopher and baseball coach, "If you don't know what you're looking for, you ain't gonna find it."

What the heck is a soul? Is it big or small? How do you measure it? What color is it? Where does it like to hang out? Does it laugh when you tickle it? How will I know it's what I'm looking for when I find it?

I logged on to enlightenedcucarachas.com and asked just these questions. Here's an excerpt from my log:

─────────────────────────────────

Cuca: It's spiritual.

Me: *Okay. What color is spiritual?*

Cuca: Spiritual doesn't have color. Spiritual is stuff you can't perceive with your eyes. Or your nose. Or any of the five senses.

Me: *Like radio waves?*

Cuca: No. Radio waves are physical. They can be detected using a radio. Spiritual is stuff that can't be observed even with a radio.

Me: *What about with a body? Can you detect spiritual with a body?*

Cuca: No.

Me: *I don't get it. If what you're saying is correct, then the soul can't be spiritual, because it has an effect on the body!*

─────────────────────────────────

I got kind of frustrated. I realized that if you want to understand what is spiritual, you have to ask one of the natives. Since I can't see angels, I logged on to one of their online tech support sites. Somehow, we managed to communicate:

Me: *Hi! You deal with technical difficulties related to spiritual/physical analog?*

Angel: Shoot.

Me: *I guess this is kind of simple. How come I can't see anything spiritual? How come I can't see my own soul? What is spiritual anyway?*

Angel: Hold it...what is it you can't see?

Me: *Spiritual. Soul. That stuff.*

Angel: And instead...

Me: *Well, instead I see physical. Matter. That kind of stuff. Something wrong with that?*

Angel: Hold on. This is neat. 'Physical matter'. Describe it.

Me: *Matter? Well, it's...it's physical. Matter. Stuff. But how about spiritual... is that real stuff or...*

Angel: I'm lacking data here. Listen: you want an answer, I want to help you, but I'm going to need some data. Now, this "physical stuff," what sort of definition does it have?

Me: *Well, let me check...I've got an online dictionary...*

Angel: No! Not that definition!

Me: *...American Heritage...*

`physical` *adj.*

```
1.a.  Of  or  relating  to  the  body,  as
      distinguished from the mind or spirit.
```

See Synonyms at bodily

Angel: No! Not a word definition. I mean, like how does it resolve?

Me: *Resolve?*

Angel: Actually, I can check that for you. Give me your ontological parameters.

Me: ?:<

Angel: What world are you in? Wait, I can check that through your IP…here it is…

HOLY, HOLY, HOLIES…LOOKY HEREY….AWESOME! Hey, how did you get through to us from way down there?

Me: *Wonders of modern technology I guess. Those guys at Chabad.org…Kabala and Java do wonders together…*

Angel: This is amazing…

Me: *I thought you guys were helping them on that…*

Angel: You've got some incredible degree of resolution down there. I mean, you've got distinct, discrete events and even discrete objects. There's exclusive resolution in your world, right?

Me: *If you say so.*

Angel: I mean, when you see something, there's nothing else in the place where that thing is?

Me: *Well, if something's there, it's like, just there. And not something else....*

Angel: Yes! **That is so awesome!** I mean, it's so totally beyond anything imaginable. And if it's there, it's not somewhere else, right?

Me: *So, about this spiritual stuff...*

Angel: **It's so cool!** The degree the Ultimate One went through to make an ultimate world! How do you beings manage to operate down there?

Me: *We're okay. Listen, I actually logged on because I had this question...*

Angel: I mean, how much information could possibly come through with so many filters and resolution encoding and all?

Me: *...so I'm trying to figure out, if there is really a soul...*

Angel: Oh yeah. Now I get it. You can't even see your own soul! **Holy cherubimis!**

Me: *Or anything that's not physical.*

Angel: WHOA! Yeah, I get it now. I mean look at those hi-res parameters. With hi-definition exclusivity and all...no, really sorry, it's actually kind of sad, there's no way you're going to be able to see the inside of anything. Look, you can't have everything...

Me: *I don't get the hi-res stuff. There's plenty of blurriness down here. I just have to take off my glasses...I still don't see any souls. Or angels.*

Angel: You're talking about spacial resolution. Hey! **That's so neat.** You guys probably have no concept of time-blur or even conceptual-blur.

Me: *Okay, hold off on the human-bashing there. That's not true. Look, we may not be angels, but we think. Ideas can get awful blurry at times.*

Angel: Hold it! You think! That changes everything…let me check the readings here…no, but your perceptors…

Me: *It's an ophthalmology issue?*

Angel: All your perceptors…eyes, ears, nose, taste, qlark…

Me: *Qlark?*

Angel: You didn't discover that one yet. And then there's haptic response…

Me: *Like touching things?*

Angel: That's the worst. They're all so hi-res. It's just how your central neurological system is designed. All the incoming data gets so tightly organized…there's just no way…

Me: *So what kind of receptors do you need to see spiritual. Maybe some of our techies could…*

Angel: Same receptors. But I think I've got it solved. It's just the degree of resolution your neurology does. Here, let's test my thesis. Hold on—how many dimensions do you do?

Me: *Uh…three?*

Angel: oy.

Me: *But this device reduces it to two.*

Angel: That's just…wild. Well, don't feel so bad, I'm in a similar situation—relatively speaking. We only do ten, but there are higher realms that do thirteen, eighteen and even twenty-six! But two, gevald. Look, we can handle it. We'll try this…

Me: *Something just popped up here.*

Angel: So what is it?

Me: *It's an angel with wings. No, wait, it's a truck. Wait, it's an angel.*

Angel: Neat, eh?

Me: *Oh, I've seen plenty of those. Old hag/young woman. Geometric figures that invert. Don't have to be an angel to make one of those.*

Angel: Yeah, but try this: Can you see both at the same time?

Me: *Ummm, well…*

Angel: Keep trying.

Me: *Yeahhhuhhnyehhhuhhh…no way.*

Angel: That's it! Your brain is designed to resolve all data to one and only one exclusive percept! That's what it's doing with everything coming into your brain. And if the brain can't resolve something…then it just doesn't exist for you. Yes! That explains it! Hold on…one more test…can you see emotions?

Me: *You don't see emotions. You feel emotions!*

Angel: oh.

Me: *You didn't know that?*

Angel: Well, there goes my whole thesis.

Me: That's a problem?

Angel: Sure, I really needed one. I could have been the first angel to discover and explain this phenomenon. But, look, if the data doesn't fit, the data doesn't fit. Doesn't matter how much you want it to...

Me: Humans aren't supposed to feel emotions?

Angel: Look, if you do, you do. I have no idea how it works. I mean, how could haptic palpation interpret better than visual...

Me: No! Not that kind of feel! I mean, feel. Like internal response. Hold on...

3. To be conscious of a specified kind or
    quality of physical, mental, or emotional
    state: felt warm and content; feels strongly
    about the election.

Angel: Ohhh! No, no, no buddy! That's conceptual! Sure, even we angels can do conceptual way beyond our own realms! No, no, no...we're talking here about I/O. Perceptor input from the outside reality! Like, you don't touch emotions with your hands, do you now?

Me: Now, that would be weird.

Angel: Sure. But do you see them with your eyes?

Me: No. Well, yes. I mean, I can see say some guy waving his arms at me and his face is all red and he's screaming bloody murder—so I know he's angry. Angry is an emotion.

Angel: But you don't see the emotion itself, right?

Me: *The emotion itself. No.*

Angel: Kewl. That's neat. You see gestures. You don't see emotions.

Me: *Angels see emotions?*

Angel: And why don't you?

Me: *Well, how could you see emotions? I mean, what could they look like?*

Angel: Look, you can't see ultraviolet either, right? Or any of the spectrum beyond that. Other creatures in your realm do. Like bees. So what do those colors look like?

Me: *But I know they are colors. I know what a color looks like. But emotions?*

Angel: You see gestures, right?

Me: *Those are physical.*

Angel: What's physical about them?

Me: *Well, a body is physical.*

Angel: A body is a concept. What makes a body separate from the background?

Me: *It moves together. As a whole.*

Angel: See. So it's a concept. Your eyes and ears take in the data, then your mind turns it into a concept. You don't see the data. You see the concept. Like, what are you looking at right now…on the 2-D screen there?

Me: *Words.*

Angel: Not little dots?

Me: *Sure, they're made of little pixels, I know that.*

Angel: But your mind doesn't see little dots. It sees words, right?

Me: *Okay.*

Angel: So, if your mind can take in data of little dots and make them into words, and it can take in data of movement and make it into an image of a body, and it can take an array of data from various optical cells and create colors out of them…why can't it form an image of emotions?

Me: *I dunno. Why not?*

Angel: That's just it! Because your mind resolves too far! Emotions can't be resolved that far! They just don't fit in! They're outside your cookie cutter. Your mind makes images only of things that are this and not that, here and not there. If it can't be resolved that far, it's lost. Unfiled. Elusive. Out of range!

Whoa…I'm overtime! Listen, come back again. Or better—send me some of your co-beings. I need to generalize this data. I mean, a larger sample. Gotta be scientific. Gotta go.

YOUR SESSION HAS BEEN ENDED. PLEASE SUPPORT ANGEL.COM WITH YOUR DONATION OF PRAYERS AND BLESSINGS.

But my search has not ended. There is more to investigate. But I'm clearly on the way. Stay tuned.

Note to the reader: For those who don't like digressions, skip to Part Six. For those who want to pummel deep into the issue of material reality, hold on tight.

Part Two: On the Couch

I admit, not everything was perfectly clear after that conversation with the angel tech-support guy. I needed a consultant to help me deconstruct this experience. Someone who knew something about the jargon this angel was babbling—"perceptors" and "resolution". I also needed a shrink. Back to surfing the Net, I found the perfect fit: A clinical psychiatrist who claimed he had experience treating angels! Over the phone, his receptionist assured me he knew a whole lot about perception issues, too. I booked, I came.

I stretched out on the therapy couch (which seemed strangely warm and showed signs of charring) and got straight to the point:

"Doc, what do you know about perception?"

Doc: You've been seeing things?

Me: *Well, not yet. Actually, it's more about what I haven't been seeing.*

Doc: Have you been under a lot of stress lately?

Me: *It's not stress. They told me it's a matter of failing to achieve resolution.*

Doc: You have an obsession with resolving matters that prevents you from perceiving…

Me: *My soul. And anything spiritual.*

Doc: Obsessive-compulsive disorder coupled with detachment from reality. Here's a prescription that you should try. Look, we could try cognitive therapy, but anything that can do, Prozac™ can do better. Start with 10 mg…

Me: *But I have a few other questions.*

Doc: It will take about two weeks to kick in. You should make an appointment now with my receptionist. There's not much point talking now, so…

Me: *Doc, hold on. I've heard you've dealt with angels before.*

Doc: Oh, no. You're not another one, are you? But you're the sunny kind, right? Say yes. Please.

Me: *Actually, I'm just a rabbi. But in my profession, I need to deal with all sorts of characters, angels included.*

Doc: My advice: Make sure you have a good property damage policy.

Me: *So they're telling me, I mean, their tech support guy is telling me, that our perceptors are messed up.*

Doc: Perceptors? That's a word? Percepts, I've heard of. Perceptors? Let me try a spell-check…

Me: *Doc, I've always had this question, but I never took psychology, so I never got to ask it. You did. You must know the answer: Is there truly a physical reality beyond human perception?*

Doc: MS Word doesn't like *perceptor*. Let me check my online therapy guide…

Me: *And what is physical, anyway? Like, how about colors? Are colors physical? I can't touch them. And my perception of them changes according to my mood. And how do I know that what others see is the same as I see? After all, all that's there is just a specific spectrum of radiant energy stimulating my rods and cones. He called it "an array of data from various optical cells."*

Doc: The Expert's Online Therapy Guide deals with perception pathologies, too. But nothing on perceptors.

Me: *All my career as a rabbi, Doc, I always thought of physical and spiritual as two completely different kinds of stuff. Like there's physical stuff you can touch with your hands and there's spiritual stuff that souls and angels are made of. But this angel tells me a different story. It seems like physical is just the surface membrane and spiritual is the depth behind it. We can't see beneath the surface. Why? Because of our perception. Because our minds don't "resolve" it.*

Doc: There's stuff here about *percepts*, but no perceptors.

> Percept: an impression of an object obtained by use of the senses.
>
> Philosophical interest in perception stems largely from questions about the sources and validity of what is called human knowledge (see <u>epistemology</u>). Epistemologists ask whether a real, physical world exists independently of human experience and, if so, how its properties can be learned and how the truth or accuracy of that experience can be determined. They also ask whether there are innate ideas or whether all experience originates through contact with the physical world, mediated by the sense organs.

Heck, what do they know? They didn't hear from the angels. If they'd just done a clinical interview with an angel or two, they'd know the whole thing is event driven.

I perked. Now I knew I had come to the right place.

Me: *Event driven? What's that mean?*

Doc: They're human interface experts, these angels. Hi-tech sector. Lucrative field. But not enough opportunities.

Me: *What's human interface got to do with any of this?*

Doc: It's a field of psychology. Ergonomics. Like when you want an end user to perform a task within a highly complex system. But you can't blow his mind with the raw mechanics of it all...

Me: *Whoa, Doc, that's just what they've been doing to me!*

Doc: So what a human interface expert does is create a layer in between the raw software algorithms and the real live human using it. Like buttons, arrows, menubars, arrows, windows, talking heads, ⌨ , ✋ , 📁 ...

Me: *But how does this layer help without getting in the way?*

Doc: Simple: It's called metaphor. The secret behind creating any world. You design objects and build an environment on the screen that's internally consistent and represents the underlying workings of the system. But it's got to be consistent. Whatever looks like a button, for instance, always acts like a button. ◀ Arrows ▶ always bring you the direction they are pointing↗. When you leave something somewhere, you come back and it's still there.

Unless it's a Microsoft human interface. Then when you come back, it's been stolen or reverse engineered.

Me: *But there aren't really any objects on the screen, right?*

Doc: Tell my secretary that. Her screen is covered with white-out.

No. There are no objects. No buttons, no arrows, no talking heads. Only events. Proof is, unplug the thing and they're all gone.

Me: *So why do we think of them as objects?*

Doc: Because they're consistent! Every time we do this, they do that. They're always in the same place and doing the same things. Our minds find it too obtuse to say, "There's a set of seemingly related events that occur consistently within the bounds of this location," and much easier to say, "That's a button."

Me: *Yes! Now I'm getting it! So all our world is just made up of events!*

Doc: Well, that's what this angel Fibo character was getting at. We put our hand out and something prevents it from going further, sending sensory information through our nervous system. Light photons stimulate our retina. Sounds waves vibrate our eardrums. Taste buds and olfactory glands sizzle. Would you like to watch an educational video while I grab a coffee?

Me: *But these events have a certain consistency within space and time...*

Doc: Well, consistent enough so that the glob of grey matter we have up there is able to organize it into...

Me: *...a world of objects!*

Doc: You've been talking to Fibo, too, right?

Me: *So Doc, this is what I really want to know: What is this "world of events" before our little minds perceive it? Is it true that our minds filter out most of what is really there?*

Doc: Fibo didn't talk much about that. But I can enter that question into this system...it's really neat. Answers just about anything you can put to a real therapist. I'd be nowhere without it.

Me: *So what does it tell you?*

Doc: Nothing. Let me try Encyclopedia Britannica.

Me: *I use that all the time. Makes me sound like a real expert rabbi.*

Doc: Me, too. Here it is:

> http://www.britannica.com/eb/article?query=perception&ct=eb&eu=119394
>
> The existence of a physical world is taken for granted among most scientific students of perception. Typically, researchers in perception simply accept the apparent physical world particularly as it is described in those branches of physics concerned with electromagnetic energy, optics, and mechanics.

That's simple. It means that the real reality is whatever the physicists tell us it is.

Me: *That's it! All I need now is to study some physics and I'll have my answer! Thanks so much, Doc!*

Doc: Just be glad you came to the expert. See you in two weeks. You have extended coverage, right?

Part Two: Rocket Science International

At first I thought, everybody knows what physics has to say: That the world is made of atoms. Neat little arrangements of little balls in the center with tiny beads zipping around them. Right?

Wrong. I checked with Rocket Science International™. Who would know better about what is reality, I thought. They gave me the full scoop in a secure, video-conference call:

Me:	*Hi, can you guys give me the full scoop on atoms?*
RSI:	Vhat kind atoms you need?
Me:	*Actually, I just want to know what they are.*
RSI:	Look, I got great deal on atomic varhead. Just smuggled now from Kazakhstan. Two Russian generals. Zey want $250,000 u.s.d.. Cheap. Zen I got French reactor…
Me:	*No, I mean what's the atom made of?*
RSI:	You asking me top secrets you asking. Vhy you need to know zis stuff? Look, it vorks, guaranteed. Okay, you vant buy top secrets, you give me another $50,000—cash on ze dash.
Me:	*Well, I don't have 50k, but maybe we can work out…*
RSI:	Okay, you in luck. Today ve make special. You get ze whole package $128.56. You can do installments…
Me:	*What about just the information? Do you have someone there who can tell me what an atom is?*
RSI:	Listen, comrade, nobody knows vhat is ze atom vhat. But it vorks, sings go boom, so vhat do ve care?

Me: *But isn't an atom something like the solar system, with beady little electrons orbiting around a clump of protons and stuff? You know, Niels Bohr, 1923?*

RSI: Haha! You Americanishe brainwash pseudo-intellectuals make me laugh! Zat's vat zey teach you in your medieval, inferior high schools! You still believe zat cute drawing like zat and all zat stuff! Zey tossed all zat in ze vaste-paper basket vhen de Broglie did scientific experiments and showed electrons are vaves—zat vas 1927! And in Russian textbooks, Vodlinsky did it in 1926, but zey wrote zat only later. Vhat you doing here in ze 21st century?

Me: *So an atom is a wave?*

RSI: Every sing is vaves. Everysing is particles. You no like it, too bad. Zey all blow up big just de same! Hahahaha…

Me: *Hold on. I thought everything is made of matter. Beady little balls of matter flying around and bouncing off each other. Like billiard balls in three dimensions.*

RSI: Matter? Vhat is matter?

Me: *Well now I don't know. What is matter?*

RSI: No sing ze matter.

Me: *Nothing?*

RSI: No sing. Ve meet at restaurant. You bring attaché case vhit twenty dollar bills…

Me: *No! I mean "matter"! Define matter.*

RSI: Vatever you say. Matter ze is concentrated energy. Ve release energy to get boom. Zis is simple relativity seory.

Me: *So what is energy?*

RSI: Energy is sings vhat happen to matter.

Me: *You're going in circles!*

RSI: Hey, you not so stupid! Okay, I vill give you example. Put your hand down on ze table. Now sell me: Your hand stops or your hand goes srew ze table?

Me: *Stops.*

RSI: Vhy?

Me: *Atoms in table hit atoms in my hand, I guess.*

RSI: Krazy amerikanishe klopheaded hamburger! Ze atoms zey are so far apart, ze table is 99.999% empty space!

Me: *So why can't my hand go right through it?*

RSI: Zat is because ze electromagnetic field vhat ze organize ze atoms from ze table, ze conflicts vit ze electromagnetic field vhat ze organize ze atoms from your hand.

Me: *But what is an electromagnetic field?*

RSI: An electromagnetic field is ze rules vhat ze particles from ze atom must to follow. Zey know: Zis many protons, only zis many electrons. No more electrons can come here. According vit zis, zey say, your hand is not allowed here. And zat is all vhat is matter!

Me: *You have a picture or something of this atom?*

RSI: You americanishe tv tube addicts alvays stuck on pikturs. You no see it, it not zere. I tell you, since Niels Bohr, nobody draws atoms no more. Ve make matrix.

Me: *Matrix?*

RSI: Okay, I explain ze matrix. Ve do also ze public service education stuff. Now vhit regular stuff, vhat you see all around you, you don't need a matrix. You can say, "Zis is here now and it is moving like zis speed so fast." Simple. So you can say `velocity x position` and zat vill equal `position x velocity`. Like zis:

`velocity x position = position x velocity`

But mit ze electrons and also ze ozer subatomic particles, you can't not say zat. Eiser you say exactly vhat is zer location or you can say vhat is zer velocity. But to say both, zis you cannot do. So:

`velocity x position` $\neq$ `position x velocity`.

So for zis you need a matrix. To make crazy matematics like zis.

Me: *You mean, these electrons are so small, we cannot measure both their speed and where they are accurately at the same time?*

RSI: No no no! You merikanishe hot dog bun head vit no meat inside! Zat is not ze idea! Ve can measure very good with finest Russian accelerators. Now for sale real cheap. But vhat I'm telling you, zat ze electron, ze does not have zis property.

Me: *Vhich, I mean which property?*

RSI: Zis property of ze having a discrete position vit a discrete velocity, both of zem at ze same time! Ze electron is not like your car, vat ze has a place and a speed and ze cop will catch you for zat. Ze electron, ze cop vill never catch him! Because or hc is not exactly in zis place where he is, or he is not moving at a speed vhat ze cop can figure out vhat is ze speed!

Me: *My car, I sort of know what that is. I don't get what this electron is. Is it a bead? A cloud? A liquid?*

RSI: Nobody knows vhat's zis electron, vhat's zis proton, vhat's no sing. All ve know is some sing, we donno vhat, is doing vhat ve donno vhat its doing. And ve know how many from zem is doing it and how many particles zey got. And how many from ze particles vill leave ven—but we can't tell you vhich one vhen.

Me: *Okay, no diagram. But at least you can give me an analogy?*

RSI: In all ze physical vorld zer is no analogy for ze atom. Like one great Russian professor, Richard Feynmanovsky I sink he vas, he said, "Ze Atom is Nature as she really is: Krazy Nuts."

Okay, I explain to you ze vave and particle sing just like Feynmanovsky explain zis sing.[9] Okay, look on your screen. Vat do you see?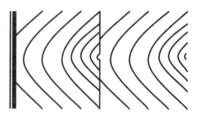

Me: *I see waves. They go through a hole. Then they're hitting a wall.*

RSI: And vat is ze vall doing?

Me: *The wave is leaving its mark on the wall. Higher in the middle, lower to the sides. That makes sense—the middle of the wave hits with more force.*

RSI: Zakly! Now look again.

Me: *I see missiles, also going through a hole—one at a time. Also hitting a wall. And the wall also gets a mark on every hit. Most of the missiles are hitting in the middle. Some to the sides. Must be a very wobbly missile launcher.*

RSI: So the vall?

Me: *The wall is recording the hits just like it did the waves. Bigger in the middle, lower towards the sides.*

RSI: Okay. So now I make ze vaves or ze missiles not to be visible. Look on ze vall. Is ziss vaves? Or missiles hitting ze vall?

Me: *Um. No clue.*

RSI: Zakly! No clue. So now ve do zis.

Me: *You just put two holes instead of one for them to go through. And now there is a pattern of marks that appear on the wall.*

RSI: That we call an *interference pattern*. Because zis comes only from interference of two sets of vaves! Like zis:

Me: *Great! So now we have a way to determine whether electrons are particles or waves!*

RSI: Zakly!

Me: *Zack who?*

RSI: Zakly we can prove!

Me: *And what exactly did Zack Lee prove?*

RSI: We prove zat ze electron is zakly both!

Me: *Huh?*

RSI: Ve prove zat if zer is no observer of ze electron going through the holes, zen ze is a vave—and ze make ze interference pattern! But if ve vill observe, like for instance ve put a little light bulb, for instance, to tell us of every time ze electron vill go through, zen ze is a particle!

Me: *That's ridiculous!*

RSI: Oh! Now I see you are understanding!

Me: *But why should electrons change from waves to particles by us watching them? They get stage fright or something?*

RSI: Ridiculous, but not so ridiculous. You see, vat is zis vave? Zis vave, as Max Born said, is not ze vave vhat you sink is a vave. Zis vave is really a set from probabilities. Probabilities of ver you vill find ze electron. Ze electron, like I said, ze has no exact place. Ze is here and ze is a little here also and no so much here, but ze is more here…

Me: *Your sounding just like that angel describing how things are in his world.*

RSI: So vit ze vave vhat ze goes through ze holes, zat is simply ze electron going through two places at once! Simple.

Me: *I get it! So when we are observing, our minds can't do that! Our minds can only see one thing or the other. Like that angel showed me with the two pictures.*

RSI: Zis is not some crazy idea vas is in ze brain. Zis is stuff from vat ve make lasers, superconductors, MRI, television sets, sis stupid video conference sing, nuclear varheads…zis is **real stuff.**

Me: *But all the real stuff I know, it sits in a certain place at a certain time and moves at a certain speed. That's what makes it physical stuff and not…I don't know what.*

RSI: Yes! Now you are getting it! Ze atom stuff is zat "I don't know vhat" stuff! Vhy? Kuz ze atom is not stuff. Nuclear varheads are stuff. Atom is mathematics. Atom is mind.

Me: *Atoms are what? But how can a physical nuclear warhead be made out of mind?*

My conversation was abruptly cut short when the CIA burst into my villa and began intense interrogation. I was never able to make contact with RSI again. But I was beginning to understand what that angel had said, that our world is "distinct, discrete events and even discrete objects." I was beginning to realize how weird it is that all this discreteness is made up of particle/waves that can't be—to use the angel's terminology—resolved.

So I kept up my research. Here's a little conversation I dug up that tells it all—almost. Phone call from Copenhagen to Berlin, 1926:

Part Four: Copenhagen, 1926

(Some background:

Neils Bohr was one of the granddaddies of quantum theory. It was under his mentorship that Werner Heisenberg (with the help of his buddies, Max Born and Louis de Broglie) trashed classic causality in order to work out the weirdness of the atom.

Erwin Schrodinger was a mature, senior physicist who was desperately trying to bring some rational calm to the situation. his wave functions turned out to be very useful—but a lot stranger than he would have liked. He ended up a committed, self-styled mystic.)

Niels Bohr: Erwin, I don't get it. Here I had a nice model that explains so much about the light spectrum, black body radiation, the periodic table of elements—all the chemists were so excited and, besides, it just looks so cool and drawable. I can see high school teachers way in the future drawing little balls in the center with beads of electrons zipping around. What are you doing messing in with your waves?

Erwin Schrodinger: Niels, you gotta be kidding. Everyone knows your model violates all the traffic laws of nature. You've taken old man Planck's quantum leaps one leap too far. Particles jumping from one orbit to another without traversing the space in between! I mean, if something can leave one place and turn up instantaneously in another, then anything could happen! And if anything could happen, then what are we scientists for?

Niels: Okay, so its weird. Life is weird, Erwin. And waves don't make it any less so.

Erwin: Oh, yeah? Waves are the classic model for all energy forms. Water waves. Sound waves. Force waves. Light waves. That's the way we've been explaining energy for years and you crazy Danes have no right to change it!

Niels: Waves in water I get. Same with waves in the air. But waves in an atom are downright ludicrous! You can't have waves without something waving, Erwin!

Erwin: *A detail. So you caught me on a detail. Look, we figured everything else out. We'll figure this one out eventually as well. The main thing is we got rid of those doggone quantum disappearing acts.*

Niels: So waves in the nothingness is okay. But disappearing acts are not. Now if that isn't arbitrary…

Erwin: *Niels, your buddy Albert already established that energy and matter are really the same stuff. So let's just do away with this whole notion of matter and tiny beads in orbit and say the whole world is made of energy. And energy is waves.*

Niels: Now there's no such thing as matter. So exactly who's going too far here? And another thing I want to know: If there aren't any electron particles, why is it my Geiger counter registers a click when they hit? Waves don't click, you know that Erwin. They splash or buzz, but they don't click. And how do you explain the whole black body radiation thing?

Erwin: *You are the one going too far, Niels. Because I know just where you're going to with all this. First you have them disappearing from one place and appearing elsewhere. Then you'll tell us they could be anywhere, their position and velocity is just an array of possibilities. And if they could be anywhere, then all of causality breaks down. I know what your pet whippersnapper student, Heisenberg, is up to, Niels.*

No longer will we be able to say that this happened because that happened. And if all those things are gone, then, gevald Niels! Why are we scientists?

Listen, Niels, electrons are energy. Energy is waves. Waves are the wave of the future. You got problems with it, go work it out. But don't go tearing down the basic laws of physics with particles that act like ghosts.

Niels: They're particles.

Erwin: *They're waves.*

Niels: Particles.

Erwin: *In the name of the Motherland, they are waves!*

Niels: Your Motherland wears army boots. Now get your tushy up here to Copenhagen and we'll have it out like men, face to face.

Erwin: *Danishes at two feet?*

Niels: Math at ten inches.

From the transcript, it seems Schrodinger took Bohr up on the deal. They did the math and after a week, poor Erwin went home feeling sick. It wasn't from the pastries.

As it turned out, these waves were even weirder than the particles. They're not waves in space, like ripples on a pond—they're happening in some abstract form of space. Something they called configuration space. Worse, each electron needs its own three dimensions. One electron on its own can be described by a wave in its 3D configuration space, but to describe another electron in the same atom, you need a whole other set of three dimensions somewhere else. With three electrons, you needed nine dimensions, and it goes on and on. Worst of all, when it comes to explaining blackbody radiation, they were back to those magical quantum leaps—when a particle moves from one orbit to another without traversing the space in between.

Schrodinger's reaction (this is for real): "If I had known we were not going to get rid of those *@&#$%^ quantum leaps, I would never have gotten involved in this business!"

It wouldn't be so bad if these were just some distant planets. But these are the things whose nutty rules are resisting your hand when you touch that table. Not that you can touch them. They're not really 'things' that you touch. Just that they have rules that don't allow your hand within their playing field. It's all very mystical. But it's been called, "the most successful theory in the history of science."[10]

These are the things that create photons out of nothing and project them at your eyeballs so that you'll think something's really there. These are the things that tickle your nose glands and tingle your taste buds. This is the stuff our world is made from.

I had one more vital piece of research to do. I had to make contact with the enlightened master of inner wisdom, decoder of quantum riddles, the wise teacher who could make brownies out of the hash I had put together from all my research, the inimitable Guadalajara Rebbe.

Part Five: Secrets of the Enlightened Master

For a question such as this, I resolved, AIM® or even iChat® wasn't going to cut it. I left my coastal villa and took upon myself the hardships of journey over the Mexican desert hills in my air-conditioned Hummer.

Upon arrival at the Guadalajaran Shteibl and Mind-Body Fitness Center, I prepared myself with the ritual immersion in the heated pool followed by the traditional shot of kosher tequila. I donned the required tunic. Then, in awe and with trepidation, I turned the doorknob of my master's private sauna and gently tiptoed in. There, in his flowing ecru cotton robes, in serene contemplation, sat the great fountain of wisdom and revealer of hidden stuff, the Guadalajara Rebbe.

Me: *Boo! Guess who?!*

Guad: Freeman! You again! Who gave you the right to hack into my personal correspondence and post these things online for public perusal!?

Me: *Esteemed master, enlightened mentor! How else will we get your teachings out there and you onto the Oprah Winfrey Show?*

Guad: But these are writings that are unfinished, incomplete, full of holes and errors! How would you like it if I took all those silly "Files" of yours and had them published for public consumption?

Me: *No, please, master! Anything but! They are so incomplete, full of holes and errors!*

Guad: Then cease and desist. And find some other way to get me on that show.

His wrath, as typical, endured but a moment. Then the air of refined composure returned to him as he spoke to me with warmth and intimate understanding.

Guad: Grab a towel and sit down. What are you here for now?

Me: I am searching for the meaning of wave/particle duality. Teach me, master, what our holy Torah says concerning this great mystery.

Immediately:

Guad: Manna.

Me: Manna?

Then a pause.

Guad: What was manna?

Me: Uh, bread from heaven that the Children of Israel consumed during their wanderings in the wilderness.

Guad: What were its properties?

Me: It was, well, according to tradition, whatever you wanted it to be. If you wanted chicken cacciatore with choco sauce, so that's what you got. You wanted potatoes and beer, so you got potatoes and beer.

Guad: How did you measure it?

Me: Measurement was an issue. You made one measurement when collecting it and you could have a lot or a little. But back home, you measured again and you had exactly one omer-measure for each member of your household.

Guad: So the manna itself, before you tasted it or measured it, what was it then?

Me: *It was, well, I guess…*

Guad: It was bread from heaven, right? So it was spiritual.

Me: *Whatever that means.*

Guad: It means that it had non-discrete properties. That is, its properties were spread over a spectrum of possibilities. Describable, perhaps, by the non-commutative mathematics of a matrix. Or by a wave function.

Me: *But then, how did we eat a wave function?*

Guad: You're sitting on a wave function right now. But don't jump, because you yourself are nothing more than a wave function. The whole of reality is nothing but wave functions, as it is called in the Kabala, "the pulsation of the isifying force."

Me: Isifying?

Guad: Isifying, vivifying…it's all the same. See Pardes Rimonim of Rabbi Moses Cordovero, "The force that vivifies is the force that isifies"—meaning, gives things their "isness," that they exist at every moment. It, too, is a wave function. A matrix of probabilities.

Me: *So how's manna different from everything else?*

Guad: Nothing. Just that the manna phenomena was out in the open, obvious for all to see what's going on. You didn't need cloud chambers or nuclear accelerators to discover the underlying reality. Manna simply ripped away the façade. It was cognitive reframing therapy in preparation to receiving the inner reality of Torah at Sinai.

Me: *Torah is about wave functions?*

Guad: Torah describes a world of probabilities—how things are in potential, before we have observed and collapsed those potential probabilities into a quantifiable reality. That is the acausality that allows for free choice: It could go this way, it could go that way—it's all up to you. But reality isn't really completely defined until you get involved.

That is why the Torah relies almost entirely on the observation of witnesses. Nothing is real in Torah until it or its effects have been observed.

Me: *Whoa! Can you run that by me again?*

Guad: Take the example of the blessing to be said in the granary at the time of harvest[11]. You're about to measure how much grain you have gathered in this year. You say a blessing thanking G–d for blessing your grain and making it plentiful. But do you have any clue what happens if you've already counted the grain?

Me: *Hey, I learned Mishna! You can't say the blessing any more.*

Guad: Why?

Me: *Because now the grain has been quantified—there's no room left for G–d's blessing. That's what it says.*

Guad: But did you think about it? Did you realize what the Mishna is saying: That before the grain was measured, it could have been more or less. It did not have a discrete measure. But now that you have measured it, you have introduced a discrete measurement to it.

Me: *Wow! Quantum physics in an ancient Mishna. It's just too weird. I don't get how we eat wave functions of probabilities. Or step on them. Or…*

My mouth ceased chattering as I noticed my master and teacher had fallen into a deep meditative state. His eyes were shut tight, his limbs did not quiver. An aura of transcendent serenity hovered over him. On the other hand, I thought, maybe he's been in the sauna too long.

Not ready to take any chances, I quickly filled a bucket with cold water and prepared to dump it onto his holy head. But at the last moment, I looked once again and saw his holy lips mumbling. I bent over to listen.

Me: *Say what?*

Guad: Mist.

Me: *I didn't even try yet!*

Guad: Throw the water upon the hot stones and there will be mist.

Me: *Oh! Mist. With a "t"!*

I did so. The temperature rose. The tequila was having its effect. Not a good combination. I sat faint on the lowest bench.

Guad: Look at your bare forearm. What do you see?

Me: *Everything's a blur.*

Guad: Look closer.

Me: *It's a pimple past a hair.*

Guad: You see beads of water forming.

Me: *Perspiration. Kewl. I'm dehydrating to boot.*

Guad: If all those beads would be perspiration, you'd be no better than a freeze-dried tortilla by now.

Me: *Master, I'm sick. I feel like a freeze-dried tortilla by now.*

Guad: Those beads are principally condensation.

Me: *Oh yeah. It's wet in here. So I'm a soggy tortilla.*

Guad: Wet? Or *humid?*

Me: *Humid. Wet. Whatever. There's a mist. An invisible mist.*

Guad: Is the mist wet before you touch it? Before it condenses on your hand?

Me: *I dunno. That's very mystical. Heh-heh. How could I tell?*

Guad: Zakly!

Me: *No! Don't bring him in here! I promised the CIA…*

Guad: He is everywhere you go…

Me: *I've been bugged?*

Guad: He is the Force of Cosmic Fusion…

Me: *What did you buy off them?*

Guad: The singular underlying reality. Only that His light progressively condenses through the medium of ten modalities of being, *the ten sefiros,* which are themselves only condensations of His Infinite Light. For all is from Him—light and darkness as well.

Me: *How did you know I had contact with RSI, anyways?*

Guad: So you see each world is an entirely new stage of condensation of that light. And with each condensation, the essential oneness becomes more concealed, more fragmented. From the World of Emanation, the light condenses to become a World of Formless Creation, and then again condenses to become a World of Form and Harmony...

Me: *I'm getting real sick.*

Guad: Until the ultimate concealment occurs in the World of Events, through the ten modalities that comprise human perception. The same ten modalities as the ten supernal sefiros, but in their most limiting, crystallized form. At this point, events become things. Objects. Illusions of a reality independent of their source.

Me: *You know about the psychiatrist, too!*

Guad: You have been searching for the secret of thingness! But there are no things! In all our holy Torah, there is no mention of things, objects, stuff...

What are things in Hebrew?

Me: *Things are just fine. Who cares that I'm melting onto your floor?*

Guad: Say "things" in Hebrew!

Me: *Dvarim.*

Guad: "Dvarim"—but that is literally words! Do you get it? In Hebrew, there are not things, only words! Cosmic events. Condensations of cosmic thoughts! That is all there is. For "He spoke and the world came into being." There is nothing else to reality but those words.

Me: *I can't find a pulse. Maybe I'm dead already.*

Guad: Only words. Dvarim. There are no things, no stuff, no matter…

Me: *It doesn't matter?*

Guad: Yes! There is no matter! At least, not as you understand matter—as an independent, self-sustaining existence of "stuff".

Me: *It doesn't matter that my corpse is about to melt into a puddle in the middle of your sauna floor?*

Guad: See! When something is important to you, you say it "matters". Words, spirit…these you say do not matter. Discard this artificial bifurcation of reality!

Me: *Bifur…Not sure what that means but I think I did it already, too.*

Guad: How do you say "physical" in Hebrew?

Me: *I need to get outa here.*

Guad: **Say physical in Hebrew!**

Me: *Um. Geshem.*

Guad: Geshem!?

Suddenly, I was struck by a cold shower from above. I looked up to see my master and teacher standing over me with an empty inverted bucket.

Guad: Geshem means "rain".

Me: *Master! You have saved me! I'm alive. I can think again!*

Guad: You mean, I have restored your spirit within you.

He threw open the door.

Me: *Spirit—"ru-ach" in Hebrew. A wind.*

Guad: And what is the relation of wind and rain?

Me: *I mean, as much as I was able to think before…*

Guad: The wind carries molecules of water, which condense to become rain. So in Hebrew, there is not such a duality of spirit and matter—only as much as there is a duality of thought and words. Or mist and moisture.

My teacher's face beamed with enlightened joy. A spirit of rejuvenation had fallen upon me. I saw that this was an auspicious time, a time when great mysteries might be revealed. Tenaciously, I prodded him further:

Me: *Master, enlighten me now, on my long and arduous quest: Reveal to me the secret entrusted to you by the heavenly transmitters of secret knowledge: What on earth is a soul?*

Guad: For this you had to contact angels, visit a quacky shrink and bring upon me a plague of Interpol, CIA, KGB and Mossad agents posing as Chassidim in my spa? You needed no more than to look in the Etz Chayim of Rabbi Isaac Luria, the Holy Ari!

Me: *oh.*

Guad: In "The Portal of Four Worlds." Portal 39, chapter 10. There you would see clearly that there are four categories of soul.

Me: *Four?*

Guad: First there is the soul of the rock, the water, the air—of all inorganic substances. This, the Ari says, is a simple, singular force that organizes the four elements…

Me: *Fire, air, water, earth.*

Guad: Which, within the current cosmological paradigm are: positive, negative, matter and anti-matter. See Likutei Sichos, volume 38, page 184. And this force integrates these four forms of events consistently as that which your senses interpret as a rock.

Me: *And organic material?*

Guad: These more complex systems demand a whole new level of creative energy and consciousness, a level that cannot be truly resolved and defined as tightly as the rock. Therefore, the plant itself does not truly resolve as a static entity, but continues to grow and change.

Me: *So animals must be a whole other level of sophistication…*

Guad: …whereby the consciousness of the cosmic creative force becomes apparent—although truly, all things are made of consciousness. But the mobility of the animal provides a modality of expression for that consciousness.

Me: *And we human beings?*

Guad: The speaking being. Here the soul of the inorganic, the organic and the animal are integrated as a harmonious whole to achieve the ultimate expression of the abstract within concrete terms. For the human, speaking being can transcend its own self to communicate with an other, to empathize, to hear its own self with another's ears, to understand itself as he is received within the other's mind. To even write crazy books that express deep mysteries in forms palatable to tv-jaded Americans.

Me: *Is that the neshama, master?*

Guad: The neshama we will not discuss now. The neshama is G–d Himself breathing within us. The Author doing a cameo. Beyond this paradigm in every way. It is neither matter nor spirit—beyond spirit more than spirit is beyond matter. So that to the neshama, both of these may as well be one and the same.

And now, my faithful nudnik disciple, you must return to your coastal villa and let these agents follow you and leave me be. And there, you will find the true meaning of all that I have revealed to you.

After a pitcher or two of spiked lemonade, washing down a few hot tamales, followed by a therapeutic session of deep tissue massage, I immediately followed my teacher's instructions and journeyed homeward. Upon arrival, I found my copy of "Sefer HaTanya" of Rabbi Schneur Zalman of Liadi mysteriously open on my desk. The following words were highlighted:

> "If the eye were granted permission to see and to grasp the spiritual vitality within each created being, then the physical, tangible stuff would not be visible at all."

The teaching of my mentor, enlightened guide, resounded in my mind: The world is made of manna. Our senses make it into white bread.

I pondered that thought as I booted up my PowerBook G5. It was then that a message appeared across my screen:

WATCH OUT! WE'RE COMING IN FOR LANDING!

A strange voice blurted something from behind me. I spun around and gasped. It was weird.

Two awesome beings with very strange goggles and earphones. Shimmering. That's right—shimmering. That's the only way I can describe it. They were there, but they seemed to be struggling to remain visible. If it weren't for those clumsy goggles covering half their faces, I'd be downright scared.

"Hi, rabbi? You're the earthly mortal who contacted me online last week, right?"

"I contacted *you*?"

The other pair of goggles turned to him. "I told you he wouldn't have a clue."

What happened next was so other-worldly, so weird, so bizarre, I'm going to need another chapter to describe it to you.

Hang in there.

Part Six: The Deal

"Rabbi, I'm from the tech-support division of Heaven Inc., and my buddy here is from marketing. You've made contact with us previously and we're here with a business proposition."

It was going in real slow. Yes, I had been thinking about souls and angels a lot lately, but mainly about why I couldn't see any such things. So now, suddenly, I was seeing angels. I thought, maybe this is my crazy imagination gone wild. But I knew there is no way I could have imagined this.

Marketing Angel: $M8^35$, this is totally awesome. If you weren't here, I'd be sure my crazy imagination's gone wild again.

Tech Angel: It's really not so nuts, $T45^2$. Everything from our realm is here. Just collapsed.

MA: Sort of like a mathematical model of reality in only three dimensions.

TA: That's kind of it. Every concept of our world exists here in analogous spatial representation. Take that object there...

They were gesturing at a rock I use as a paperweight on my desk.

TA: That's one of the thoughts generated by $H290^5$.

MA: I always knew that angel was a little inert.

TA: His thoughts are, too. So, here, they look like this. J_265, on the other hand, has thoughts like that one there. A little more dynamic.

Now they were pointing at the potted plant by the window.

MA: And whose thoughts are those ugly critters?

I knew they'd get to the cockroaches at some point. Very embarrassing.

TA: You don't want to know, T45^2.

MA: Totally Cool. Each thought, laid out, distinct and separate from the other.

TA: And there are creatures here, conscious ones, to whom this is reality.

MA: You mean they get to see all our thoughts? Right out in the open like this?

TA: They have no clue what they're looking at! They think these things are just here and that's it. That's what he contacted me about: He called it 'physical'.

MA: Which means?

TA: I figured out what that means. It means when you see just this highly resolved representation of an idea, but you can't see the idea behind it. So you're left with this highly fragmented, super-static…well, this stuff.

MA: Hey, I'm an angel and I also can't see what's behind it. How do you do that? How did you get the simulation so real-like?

TA: That's the whole trick. That's what these goggles and all the gear are all about. They block out all the depth of the signal and provide only the final, resolved, outer stimuli.

MA: What a trip! Space becomes so awesomely heavy. You have to pass through it one place at a time. And time trudges forth step by step. Hey, look at this!

Now he's waving his hand slowly in front of his eyes. Then the other guy starts doing it. I'm telling you, these angel characters...

MA: W h o a ! K E W L ! First it's in one place, then in another, then in the next...

TA: This is what I wrote about in my thesis. Discrete time-space. Extreme-resolution of both velocity and position.

MA: That was a thesis. This is for real. I'm telling you, $M8^3 5$, this is going to be the next big wave in angel tourism.

TA: But we need someone at this end. The tour guide.

MA: So we got this mind-directed entity here—but isn't he stuck in the same protocol? I mean, how could anything possible *think* down here?

TA: No, there's mind there. I mean, he managed even to contact us. Looks like there's something there transcendent of...

By now, I got the clue that they were discussing yours truly. And they weren't being very nice about it.

Me: *Hold on, gentlemen, this is my office. And if you're going to be making visits to this place, you're going to have to learn a little of earthling protocol. Like proper etiquette. Like about talking about people to their face...*

MA: W o w ! Willful consciousness. Even some personal sensitivity.

Me: *You guys don't get it, do you?*

TA pulled something out of MA's mouth gear. MA fluttered a lot, not very happy.

TA: Rabbi, please excuse my co-agent here. This is all very new to him. Actually, we're very sensitive to…

Me: Let's get past the excuses. Now, just explain to me what this is all about. What's the deal? And what's it going to cost me?

MA grabbed that piece of hardware back and was now able to talk again.

MA: Umm. TA, how do I explain this, TA?

TA: The space travel line.

MA: Right, space travel. The deal is like this, rabbi. You know all about space travel. You do that all the time, with—umm—how many wings does this…never mind, we know you do that. You can basically move about any direction at will, right. M8^{3}5, you better have provided clean data here. Now, how about time travel? A little more locked in, eh? Most of the time, you go only one direction. It takes a lot of work to jump in and out of the various time frames and…

TA: No! I told you, they're stuck in the causal-linkage mindset here! They don't do time-travel because they think it's linear and all!

MA: But you told me they think, right?

TA: Just get on with the presentation.

He's back to me now.

MA: But the biggest challenge has always been ontological travel. I mean, at least with time, you move somewhere. But in realms of reality, it's just so static. You're projected by the Cosmic Mind into a realm of being and you're just stuck there throughout that phase of existence. No upwards, no downwards, just stuck. Now, here I don't know, but where I come from, we know there's something beyond and below. I mean, where I come from, angels are just *dying* to get out of there. Hey, M8^{3}5, *dying* to get out of there! Hey that's a pun if I ever heard one! *Dying…*

TA: The guy's standing there, waiting for your pitch…

MA: He's cognizant, right? Do you think he's getting this?

Me: I'm getting the whole thing. Let's get down to business…

MA: Tour guide. You.

Me: 20% commission. Stock options. Benefits package.

MA: We can guarantee supernal revelations of the first order delivered to your consciousness after three successful tours.

TA: Hold it! We can't talk business yet! There has to be a basic understanding of how the system works! T45^2, what happened to your standard line of marketing ethics? "Our job is education, not sales." You enter a lower realm and the ethics are out the window, eh?

Me: Tell me, can we do this in reverse? Can I get humans up there with this device?

I must have said something real bad. They looked pale and fluttery. I thought I saw sparks.

MA: oy.

TA: Rabbi. No. Please. You could overcharge. That's ugly. You don't want to. Rabbi, let me explain the whole thing and you'll understand why.

276

Me: *If I video-tape this, will it come out?*

I started setting up the camera while he was talking. Never did get an answer. The tape is real weird. You can watch it.

TA: It's really not so hard, because we can provide an analogy from your own psyche. You see, in fact, you are doing ontological travel all the time—whenever you speak, in fact. Or any other form of congruent expression.

MA: He does that. It's true. He talked, for example.

The digital zoom on the camera was doing weird things.

TA: You recall our conversation. That your perceptors are stuck in an extreme mode of resolution. From that arises this phenomena that you first contacted me to discuss. You call it…

Me: *Physical.*

TA: Right. Actually just a highly discrete description of reality. Problem is, with such hi-definition, all meaningful context is lost and your entire world may appear void of inner expression. As though it's just autonomously here. All on its own.

MA: Hey, yeah! It's just like that! Like it's just here. All on its own! Excellent description!

TA: Unless you have the code.

MA: We have the code. You sign the NDA and we can throw that into the deal.

TA: Now, the interesting thing is that human beings such as you are capable of decoding these things. If you've ever read *The Adam Files*, you'll know what I'm talking about. In fact, we only have the code because we've built on that original work of the first human being, Adam.

Me: *You mean, the Hebrew language?*

TA: We're getting side-tracked. The point is that you have a mental protocol by which you can re-conceive these hi-definition percepts into abstract concepts. And you can also work in reverse, translating abstract concepts and emotions into discrete language and words.

At this point, there was a screen up in the room. I remember that for sure. Okay, it doesn't come out in the video. But it was there.

TA: Specifically, your mind is constantly traveling back and forth through five distinct realms, each separated by a quantum leap of reality. They are:

realm	relates to...
Intellect	The World of Emanation, Top Floor
Emotions	The World of Emanation, Main Floor
Thought	The World of Primal Creation
Speech	The World of Formation
Articulated Words	The World of Events

Me: *I need an example.*

TA: Here's an example: Take a single word. Like "dream". Say it over and over...

Me: *dream, dream, dream...*

TA: Until it becomes just a sound.

Me: *...dream, dream, dream...*

TA: Because that's all it is. No meaning, just a hollow event.

Me: *...dreamdreamdreamdreamdream...*

TA: Something like your world.

MA: Just seems to be here. And that's it.

TA: But when that sound is in the context of speech, whoa, then it gets meaning. It becomes part of something greater. It becomes a word, a message. Like an angel—angels are messages from above.

Me: *So speech—that's like the world you come from?*

TA: Sort of. It's what you were looking for when you asked to see the soul of things. In your world, you see just the end results. In ours, you see the consciousness behind them. Like, say, a chemical reaction.

Something popped.

TA: Or an electric current.

Something zapped.

TA: Or a plant growing.

The plant blossoms burst out.

TA: Or the neurological processes of one of these ugly creatures walking across your table.

Something v e r y weird...never mind.

TA: Down here, you just see what's happening. In our world, we see a consciousness, an idea. Because of that idea, the electrons know where to move, the plants know how to grow and the little bugs know how to crawl. We angels are all absorbed in the idea, so much so, we don't perceive this artifact you call the physical body.

Me: *So how do I get there?*

TA: But there are higher worlds. Like there is something higher than speech.

Me: *Higher than speech?*

TA: Sure. C'mon, what comes before speech

Me: *Uh…dinner?*

MA: Dinner?

Me: *Best before dessert, so people don't leave.*

TA: Thought comes before speech.

Me: *If I have time. But thinking is hard.*

TA: Thinking is harder, but on the other hand, speech is very frustrating compared to thought. Because, in thought, words aren't so distinct one from the other. You hardly feel the words at all, because the context and meaning is so clear up there. The words are like letters carved out on shiny jewels—you can't see them for the light that's shining. And that's what makes them so, so much more powerful. A thousand words of speech can never express what a single word of thought has to say.

Me: *So, before I make a speech, I'm supposed to think about it? They didn't put that in my contract.*

TA: Once they get down to words, they have to resolve clearly. Each word has to have its particular meaning. It has to be this and not that. The context, the light, it all gets lost.

Me: *You're saying that I'm supposed to think about it, but I'll never be able to really say what I was thinking. So I'm doomed to be misunderstood.*

MA: Listen, we're not doing a Toastmasters™ session here! This is about worlds, remember. He's trying to explain to you the World of Thought, i.e. Yetsira.

Me: *Okay, so that's the place I want to get to. That's the deal. Don't call your lawyer and I won't call mine.*

TA: So, there are worlds of thought. Where things barely know that they exist. But then, there's something even higher than thought. The place where those thoughts are coming from. The inner structure of the psyche. Not what it's doing, but what it *is*.

MA: Why are you so hung up on going up to those higher worlds?

Me: *It's just a gut feeling. A yen, deep inside. It's who I am.*

TA: Right. Emotions are where words come from, but there are no words in emotions. It's a whole different reality there. And the same with emotions compared to intellect.

MA: He hasn't a clue what you're talking about.

Me: *Not true. I'm getting it. It's like the sound of the word 'dream' compared to the sentence 'I had a dream' compared to the whole thought that you get when you hear the whole speech, compared to the powerful emotion behind that speech, compared to the whole mindset it took to come out with that speech. Five levels of reality.*

MA: I'm impressed.

TA: Four worlds. The last two are in the highest world. Atzilus.

MA: Whoa! ATZILUS! WHAT A HIGH!

Me: You have angels up there, too?

MA: What a riot! **Angels in Atzilus!** This guy's for real isn't he? I love it!

TA: No angels anywhere in proximity. Atzilus is pure G–dliness. I mean, that's The Source. Only neshomos come from there. Most step down somewhat as they descend. There are those that don't even do that. But even when they do descend, it's not like with angels. They retain that transcendent Atzilus quality in their descent.

Me: Neshomos? That's what I was calling to ask you about...

TA: You called to ask about why you can't see spiritual. Which means you know what that is. So your perceptors are here, at what you call physical, but conceptually you can perceive the higher image. The soul inside each thing.

Me: Like my neshama?

TA: We're not talking about neshamos now. That's Atzilus stuff. We're talking about spiritual. The soul inside each thing.

The marketing guy got really impatient and pushed his cohort aside.

MA: All he's trying to get at is that you'll be the perfect tour guide. Because you can connect the different realms, see. Now, for the benefits package, I can work out an eternal life scheme…

Me: *But the neshomos bit—you didn't get to that…*

TA: Neshomos don't fit into this whole scheme.

MA: No, we won't be bringing any neshomos into this. No need. They travel back and forth, free of charge all the time.

TA: Neshomos are different. They come in as a supplement. There's a being there already, with its own soul, and then the Cosmic Master breathes into it. Direct. And then that body starts acting with this different type of consciousness. Entirely transcendent. Traversing all worlds.

MA: That's why we don't have to bring those here.

Me: *But I have a neshama.*

There was a pause. I was honestly thinking maybe they had come unplugged. Then the marketing guy talks real slow and softly:

MA: He   says   he   has   a   neshama.

TA: I didn't tell you about that?

MA: I'moutahere.

TA: Heck, don't worry! It's a real stepped-down signal. It's not like we're talking about some tzadik or something. They call him the rabbi, but he's really pretty out-there.

MA: He's got a neshama.

TA: That's what makes him a tour guide, see? He can traverse—at least conceptually.

This was my chance. I grabbed it.

Me: *That's right. You guys can come down here, and you haven't even got a neshama. Just funny goggles. I have a neshama and I want to go up there. And that's the deal.*

MA: But look what you've got down here! You gotta be **c r a z y** ! *This* is the ultimate trip!

Me: *That's nonsense!*

TA: No, it's true! You may be missing a lot of contextual data down here, but you have the Divine Mind in hi-definition, kinetic-tactile...

Me: *The ultimate trip is what you guys are describing, up there. Worlds of Speech. Worlds of Thought. Higher Being and Consciousness. I want it and I want it now!*

TA: But, rabbi, it'll blow your little consciousness to pieces! You won't be able to return to your corporeal state! You're just not ready!

Me: *Who needs a corporeal, anyway?*

MA: We do. For a tour guide.

TA: The Supreme Consciousness. He wants you to have one. And He's the Boss. We can't do anything to abrogate our contract with Him. You know what would happen to us? I mean, if we would even *think* about such a thing, we would immediately...

Those were the last words. I know it wasn't a hallucination, because the whole building had a power-out when they—whatever it was that happened to them. Don't make me describe it. They were gone.

Okay, I blew it. Maybe I pushed too far. Maybe I haven't really gotten to the bottom of this soul stuff, either. There's a lot of mainstream, scientifically accepted stuff already out there. Like Sir John Eccles and David Chalmers and others—do a search and find out for yourself: Human Consciousness Research. As for what I've written here, you'll find the basic idea in Likutei Sichot, volume 6, pages 109–118, in Tanya and all throughout chassidus.

But ever since those angels left, the world doesn't look quite the same anymore. I haven't squished one of those angelic ideas on my desk since. Funny, though, how one of them just turned over and died the instant that marketing angel flickered out...

Kategor, Sanegor$_1$ and Sanegor$_2$
Attorneys at Law
A6FF;98E4;99DE;FFFF
World of Supernal Litigation

WITHOUT PREJUDICE

BY REGISTERED MAIL

Tammuz 22, 5764

Rabbi T. Freeman
Ground Floor
World of Assiya

Dear Rabbi Freeman,

I represent Heaven Inc.

It has come to the attention of my client that you are persisting in your attempts to distribute the so-called "Files" for educational purposes in the mainstream market.

As counsel for Heavenly Inc., I am putting you on notice that such unauthorized action may result in legal proceedings under the Classified Documents Act, 5764. This Act was recently proclaimed in force by the Heavenly Body of Legislature. As you are undoubtedly aware, the Heavenly Body of Legislature, in its infinite wisdom, set out in subsection 18 (9) that the provisions of this Act prevail over the provisions of such other Act and over regulations, rules or by-laws made under such other Act which conflict therewith, unless otherwise expressly provided.

If you wish to avoid legal proceedings, my client advises that a consensual resolution may be reached through payment of a royalty schedule of 50% on a quarterly basis.

If I do not receive a satisfactory response within 30 days of the above date, I will take whatever action is appropriate.

Govern yourself accordingly.

Yours truly,

D. Sanegor$_2$

About the Author

Tzvi Freeman was born in Vancouver, Canada, where he became involved at an early age in Yoga, Tao and radical politics. In 1975, he left a career as a classical guitarist and composer to study Talmud and Jewish mysticism for nine years. He received rabbinical ordination at the Lubavitch Central Yeshiva in New York and completed post-graduate studies at the Rabbinical College of Canada.

Every day, Chabad.org mails out a 'Daily Dose of Wisdom' written by Tzvi Freeman, as well as a semi-weekly, in-depth analysis of a topic in Jewish mysticism. His previous two books, *Bringing Heaven Down to Earth* and *Be Within, Stay Above*, are collections of meditations based on the teachings of "the Rebbe," Menachem M. Schneerson. *Men, Women & Kabala* is a collection of thoughts from Kabalists throughout the centuries.

Rabbi Freeman is also a published expert, consultant and lecturer in the field of educational technology, having held posts at the University of British Columbia and Digipen School of Computer Gaming. He has also written feature articles for Game Developer Magazine and lectured on game design for Digipen School of Computer Gaming. He authored the award-winning CD ROM, "A to Zap!" which was featured as 'Hot Pick of the Year' on Good Morning America. In the year 2000, he was appointed to the educational advisory council of Vivendi Interactive in recognition of his work in early childhood user interface.

Rabbi Freeman currently resides in Thornhill, Canada with his wife, Nomi, and their children.